Sarah Cobb

Other books by Catherine M. Rae

Brownstone Facade
Julia's Story

CATHERINE M. RAE

Sarah Cobb

ST. MARTIN'S PRESS

NEW YORK

n|90

Design by Judith A. Stagnitto

Library of Congress Cataloging-in-Publication Data

Rae, Catherine M.
      Sarah Cobb / Catherine M. Rae.
          p.   cm.
      ISBN 0–312–04579–4
      I. Title.
      PS3568.A355S27 1990   90-8612
      813'.54—dc20   CIP

First Edition: September 1990
10 9 8 7 6 5 4 3 2 1

For David and Mary Louise Rae
and for Larry Ricciardi

ACKNOWLEDGMENTS

For their help in the preparation of this novel I am grateful to Dr. Barbara Perina, Dr. Alan Gans, and Penelope Colby. My special thanks go to Gene Rae and Anne Savarese, my husband and my editor, for their patience and support.

PART ONE

Millicent Cobb

1

Since I am alone a good part of the time these days, I have ample opportunity to think about the past, to dwell happily on the glorious moments, and to shudder at the tragic ones. I have to be careful, though, when in the company of other members of the family, not to let anything slip, in fact, to monitor my speech. I've had plenty of practice doing that, however, having realized while I was still quite young that it was unwise to voice opinions that did not coincide with those of my elders, and that emotion (of almost any sort) had best be kept hidden.

Appearance was what counted in New York in the 1870s and 1880s, while reality, or perhaps I should say the truth of the matter, was subservient to "how things would look," and woe betide him who did not abide by that dictum. Not surprisingly, such an attitude led inevitably to the development of some of the less admirable traits of character: secretiveness, mistrust, even deceit. I should know; I have seen enough of it over the years.

I have often thought the struggle to keep up the pretense that all was well may have been responsible for the sudden rages to which my sister, Agatha, was subject when we were young. Poor clumsy Aggie! What she wanted to be and what she was were poles apart. I remember seeing her pore over the fashion magazines, *Godey's Lady's Book* and others, looking longingly at the pictures of slim-waisted models in long, graceful gowns, and hearing her sigh as she closed the book. She knew full well that neither the expensive silks (sometimes twenty yards of material went into one of our afternoon dresses) and laces that Mama purchased, nor the skill of the seamstress who came to the house could transform her into a beauty. She was only two years my senior, but looked far older. She had a large frame, like Papa and our brother, Henry, but not their fine features; hers bordered on being coarse, the nose too big, the chin too heavy, and the small eyes set too close together. Her hair, a lovely reddish brown, silky and naturally wavy, should have helped, but somehow it didn't. I don't think she had the patience to arrange it properly.

I am sure it became apparent to her early in life that she would never be sought after, and I am equally sure that in return, or in defiance, she pretended not to care. The stiff, overbearing, and frequently rude attitude she adopted in an effort to cover up her feeling of inferiority were most unattractive, but not as upsetting as her sudden outbursts of rage. Whenever these "spells," as Papa called them, occurred, I, for some reason I never understood, was the only one who could calm her. She wasn't violent (although that was what we all feared she would become); she didn't lash out or throw things, but would shout, "No! No!" or "Why? Why?" and hammer with clenched fists on the nearest chair or table while tears streamed down her face. If I waited a moment or so and then gently stroked her hair or rubbed the back of her neck while humming or crooning softly in her ear, the shouting would change to a series of moans, which would gradually cease altogether. Mama tried the same procedure in vain; Aggie would brush her off roughly, and then Mama would cry.

It happened one night when Aunt Carrie, Mama's younger sister, and Uncle Jim Curtis were at the table with us in the gloomy dining room of the Tenth Street house, and I thought Papa was going to strike Aggie. He had no patience

4

whatsoever with these "spells," and more than once threatened to have Aggie put in an asylum if she couldn't control herself. I knew he never would, though; he would have been too afraid of disgracing the family name. His threats, however, must have frightened Aggie, for after a while she *did* learn to control herself. Or maybe she outgrew the ailment; I don't know.

I didn't mean to write so much about Aggie, but since our lives were so closely entwined by virtue of proximity, I have found it impossible not to do so. I never liked her, and I doubt that my parents did, but of course we pretended—oh, those pretenses! But we had to tolerate her; what else was there to do? Henry had little to do with her while we were growing up; he must have liked me better, because I remember his teaching me to play backgammon, and occasionally taking me for a ride on the horse cars. But I think that was only when he had nothing better to do.

After our parents died, Mama of a stroke in 1885 and Papa of pneumonia the following year, Henry inherited everything (with instructions to provide for Aggie and me until we married). He lost no time in marrying Maria Winslow and setting her up in style in a house on Forty-ninth Street, two doors down from Fifth Avenue.

As soon as Henry left, Aggie declared herself mistress of the family home, a position that gratified her desire for authority, and one that I never contested. Running that dark, cheerless house held out no appeal for me at all.

As a girl, I used to visit friends in the immediate neighborhood, daughters of families acceptable to Mama and Papa, and it seemed to me that without exception, their homes were far more pleasant than ours. The Hawksworth house, for instance, had deep, comfortable chairs and sofas covered in flowered chintz, airy lace curtains that filtered the light, and bright touches of color in the pictures and ornaments, a sharp contrast to our dull, scratchy mohair furniture, brown velour hangings, and grim portraits of bygone

Cobbs. And Eleanor Hawksworth, who was just my age, was allowed to invite as many as she liked for tea.

I particularly liked visiting Louisa Grinnell, over on Lexington Avenue, where afternoon tea was a noisy, informal affair in front of a blazing fire in the back parlor, and where no one was ever admonished to sit up straight or to be careful not to take too much sugar. Mrs. Grinnell was a large, comfortable woman, obviously adored by her six children and her ruddy-faced husband. She never seemed to be out of sorts, and the only time I saw her even slightly cross was when Tom, the youngest boy, tied an old shoe to the cat's tail. That was over in a moment, however, and as soon as the shoe was removed, Tom was sitting next to his mother on the sofa, looking only mildly chagrined.

When it was time for me to leave—and how I hated to exchange the chatter and laughter of that parlor for the hushed solemnity of ours—one of the older boys would see me home, carefully taking my arm at the crossings. I was only fifteen or sixteen at that time, and came into contact with few of the opposite sex, but at eighteen, when I put my hair up, I was allowed to attend various Assembly dances and charity balls, more often than not chaperoned by my parents. Aggie refused to appear at these functions on the grounds that the music and the heat gave her a headache. At least that was what she said; we all knew the real reason was that she wanted to avoid the humiliation of spending the entire evening sitting on a fragile gilt chair with an empty dance card on her wrist, trying to act as if she didn't care.

I did not have that problem, probably because I was slim, of average height, like Mama, and danced well. A picture of me taken about that time shows that I had regular features, a somewhat high forehead, arched eyebrows, and a rather skeptical expression. By no means beautiful, but pretty enough so that I did not lack partners. Martin Grinnell, Louisa's oldest brother, was particularly attentive, and in the spring of 1883 he asked Papa for my hand. He was refused:

6

Papa did not think he was well enough established in business to support me properly. I was not really disappointed; I wasn't in love with Martin, but I think I might have been willing to marry him if only to get away from the jurisdiction of my parents. Who knows, though? I might have been miserable.

I was worried for a while that Papa might marry me off to Clayton Bushwick, an older man who looked like the pictures of General Grant, and always smelled of cigars. I noticed that he eyed me appraisingly whenever he called or came to dinner, and each time that happened I could not help shuddering. The thought of being touched by those thick, hairy fingers that toyed constantly with the heavy gold watch chain looped across his protuberant stomach was too abhorrent to contemplate. Fortunately he and Papa, and on occasion Henry, lingered so long over their port and cigars after the ladies had withdrawn that I was able to leave the parlor and escape to my room before they appeared. I think Mama must have known how repulsive I found the man, since she never made any objection to my departure. It is also possible that she spoke to Papa, causing him to refuse any offer Mr. Bushwick may have made, because after a while he stopped coming. Aggie apparently missed his visits; I once overheard her say to Mama that she thought he was a "fine figure of a man." Dear me!

2

It seemed as if Aggie and I were in mourning forever, first for one parent and then the other, wearing nothing but unadorned black, which I hated, and which did not become me. It suited Aggie, though, and she continued to wear dark colors long after it was necessary. I think it made her feel virtuous, as did her careful management of the funds with which Henry provided us. She spent hardly anything on clothes for herself, and bought the cheapest aprons and uniforms she could find for the maids. Those poor maids! Aggie reduced their wages from fifteen dollars a month to twelve, saying that Mama had been overpaying them. The only thing she did not economize on was food, but then Aggie always loved to eat heartily. Once when I asked her what she intended to do with the money she was saving she smiled slyly to herself before answering.

"You never know, Millie," she said finally. "Henry might go bankrupt, or he might die and leave everything to Maria. We don't want to become paupers, do we?"

Of course, that was ridiculous; she knew as well as I did that after Papa's death Henry had set up trust funds for us, and that even if he did go bankrupt; we would still have the income from them. Aggie is becoming miserly, I thought, not knowing then that such a trait in her character would prove useful to me later.

* * *

In accordance with the custom of the times, we lived quietly
during the year that followed Papa's death, neither entertaining nor going out in society. Consequently, in the late winter
of 1886, when the period of mourning was officially over, I
felt rather out of things. Besides, my two closest friends,
Eleanor Hawksworth and Louisa Grinnell, had married in
the interim, and moved uptown. I saw them occasionally,
but it wasn't like old times; they were wrapped up in their
own affairs, and moved in different circles, as newly married
couples are apt to do.

We dined with Henry and Maria once in a while, but those
occasions were strictly *en famille*; I suppose Henry was afraid
to invite any of his colleagues or business friends for fear
Aggie would embarrass him. It was obvious to me that we
were asked out of a sense of duty, not out of warmth or
affection, and even though Maria was an excellent hostess, I
did not enjoy myself. Aggie did, though; the food was
always plentiful and delicious.

I wasn't enjoying myself in general; I did not like the way
I was filling in my days with trivialities, wandering up and
down the Ladies' Mile, shopping for things I didn't need,
taking walks in the park, or having tea by myself at the Astor
House or the Fifth Avenue Hotel. I thought that perhaps I
would like to travel, see the treasures of Paris or Rome, but
I was too timid to go alone, and I certainly did not want my
sister for a companion. In any case, Aggie was perfectly
content with things as they were; indeed, she seemed happier
than I'd ever seen her, devoting her mornings to household
affairs, ordering the servants about, checking up on them,
remonstrating, scolding, and making up the day's menus.

I must say she kept busy: afternoons and certain evenings
were given over to activities and meetings in connection with
the Women's Christian Temperance Union, of which she had

recently become a staunch supporter. In the past, liquor had been served, albeit infrequently, in our house; Papa had kept a modest supply of claret, sherry, Madeira, and port on hand for special occasions, but after his death, Aggie poured it all out, to the astonishment of the Irish cook.

The seldom-used back parlor became her office; she had Henry's old desk brought down from upstairs, and placed it so that the ladies on her committee could arrange themselves in a semicircle facing her as she sat behind it. The large credenza against the wall was emptied of Mama's Dresden shepherds and maidens to make room for tracts on the evils of drink and communications from Frances E. Willard and other members of the National Prohibition Party. To please Aggie, I attended one of her meetings, but I was so appalled by the uncompromising intolerance I heard expressed by those determined women that I never went again. I suppose they did some good, and control of the rampant drunkenness of the time was certainly a worthy cause, but I think that had I been a drunkard and seen one of those viragos coming toward me waving a pamphlet, I would have turned and fled. As it was, I did flee the house on afternoons that meetings were held, even when I had no errand or specific goal in mind.

I did not like to venture too far afield, but some days I would walk up to Fourteenth Street and board a train on the Third Avenue elevated line, and ride as far north as the Bronx before returning to lower Manhattan. The little wooden passenger cars were not crowded early in the afternoon, and I was nearly always able to secure a seat next to a window. When viewed from below, the El was anything but an architectural delight; the iron framework on which the tracks were laid was ugly, dirty, and rusty, and the small steam engines left a trail of soot and cinders, which sifted down to the already littered cobblestones below, causing pedestrians to scatter. It was exciting at times, though; twice I saw horses bolt and almost upset the heavy wagons they were pulling. I do not know whether the noise of the trains frightened them, or whether they were struck by the hot cinders, but I remember being frightened myself the first time I saw it happen, and running into a little fruit and vegetable store to be safe from the hooves of the brewery horses.

The view from the windows of the elevated train as it steamed uptown fascinated me; at times we seemed to be so close to the tenements that lined Third Avenue for part of the trip that I felt as if I were spying on the private lives of the inhabitants. Further on we'd pass open fields, some of which contained makeshift shacks that looked far too fragile to withstand the wind and the rain, and then, surprisingly, a row of neat red brick houses, each with a tiny, well-tended garden in front of it, all parts of a New York I had never known existed.

On other days I would take the Fifth Avenue stage up to Eighty-second Street, past the mansions of the Vanderbilts and Astors, and spend an hour or two in the new Metropolitan Museum of Art, a restful place, where one could sit down and admire the works of the masters without being disturbed. I've had a warm feeling for the museum over the years, to be expected, I suppose, in view of what happened there one afternoon in March 1887.

3

The weather was so unexpectedly lovely that day that I left the museum earlier than usual, intending to walk part of the way down Fifth Avenue before taking the stage to Tenth Street. As I started toward the exit I noticed a fairly large group of people gathered in front of Rosa Bonheur's painting entitled *The Horse Fair*, which Mr. Cornelius Vanderbilt had recently given to the museum, but no one was in the next gallery, where Vermeer's *Young Woman with a Water Jug* was on display, fortunately at eye level. (At that time the practice was to hang paintings one above the other to the top of the red-baize-covered walls, making it difficult to appreciate the uppermost ones.) I don't know how long I stood there entranced with the magic of light and color in the masterpiece, but I do know that it was only with an effort that I tore myself away from it.

The dreamy mood the painting engendered in me persisted as I went down the wide marble steps and made my way slowly out of the building, which is probably why I did not see the ragged little street urchin until it was too late. He was disappearing around the corner of the building, clutching my tapestry purse almost before I realized what had happened.

A moment later a young man I had noticed earlier in the portrait gallery shot down the stone steps and ran after the small figure, calling, "Stop, thief!" as he went. He returned shortly, shaking his head ruefully, and panting slightly.

"I'm very sorry, ma'am," he said, looking down at me with some concern. "He was completely gone—evaporated—by the time I turned the corner. May I be of any assistance?"

When I said I was unharmed, and that I could easily walk home instead of taking the Fifth Avenue stage, he begged to be allowed to escort me to my door in a hansom cab. I thanked him, and said that he was very kind, but that I enjoyed walking in the fine weather. He looked disappointed, but bowed politely and said nothing further. He must have been watching me, though, for when a hole in the pavement caused me to turn my ankle and stumble against the railing at the side of the path, he was beside me in an instant.

"You can't possibly walk any distance now. I insist that you permit me to see you safely home," he said sternly, supporting me with one hand and signaling to the driver of a hansom cab with the other. I must have looked rather uncertain, because he smiled suddenly, and assured me that he had only my welfare in mind.

"Who was that who brought you home in a hansom?" Aggie demanded as soon as I entered the house. "And what is wrong with your foot?"

She was not at all sympathetic when I finished giving her a brief account of the incident.

"You should have learned by now to have a firm grasp on your purse at all times, Millie. How much money did you lose?"

"Only a few dollars," I answered. "Not enough to worry about, but probably enough to feed that poor child for two or three days."

"Nonsense! Don't be sentimental, Millie. It's more than likely that his drunken father sent him out to steal money for liquor."

I stopped listening as she carried on about the morals, or the lack of them, of the poor, and let my mind dwell on the events of the past hour. In spite of my painful ankle, the ride downtown had seemed all too short; I had been completely at ease in my rescuer's presence, not even a bit flustered at the way his glance kept returning to my face, as if to study it.

He introduced himself as John Townsend, and said he was in New York on business in connection with the Boston Museum of Fine Arts, where he was employed in their legal department. He had been conferring with Mr. John Taylor Johnston, the president of the Metropolitan, that afternoon.

"I like your city," he said, gesturing toward the early greenery of Central Park on the right, and then toward the impressive facades of the limestone mansions on the left. "It's a city of contrasts, of the unexpected. I find it all tremendously exciting, and have been trying to see as much of it as I can in my spare time. I even went up to the top of the Equitable Building to get an overall view."

"You might like the view from the elevated line," I said. "It varies so much as one rides along." And I described some of the sights that had interested me. I do not remember our entire conversation—I think we talked about points of interest, the Brooklyn Bridge, the Statue of Liberty, the ferry boats—but I shall never forget the strength of the arm that assisted me from the carriage and up the steps to my front door. And I remember well the slight pang I felt when he relinquished his hold on me as the maid opened the door.

I had trouble sleeping that night, not because of the pain in my ankle, which by that time was minimal, but because I kept seeing his face, hearing his voice, and feeling the warmth of the hand that held mine when he said good-bye.

I did not dare hope to see him again; he'd said nothing about calling, but when flowers arrived the next afternoon with a note wishing me a swift recovery, my heart leapt. Suddenly the whole world looked brighter, even in the spring rain that was falling outside as I set the vase of flowers in the parlor windows.

He came the next evening, to inquire about my ankle, he said. Thank goodness Aggie had gone around the corner to one of her meetings; she never would have left me alone with him, or she might have frightened him off. As it was, the evening was perfect, from the moment he came into the room until he left about two hours later. Almost immediately we settled down to talk like old friends, an unusual occurrence on such short acquaintance. I rang for tea and biscuits, wishing I could offer him Madeira or sherry, as I had known Mama to do when someone called unexpectedly. I had lighted the gas logs earlier against the chill of the rainy night, and after he drew up a chair, positioning it so that we could converse with ease, I had the feeling that our ordinarily drab parlor had been pervaded by an atmosphere of warmth and coziness. Perhaps it was his presence, or the look in his eyes when his gaze lingered on me . . .

In answer to my inquiry about his lodging, he told me he was staying at the Osborne, that magnificent new apartment building on Fifty-seventh Street, with a cousin who lived there.

"How long will you be in New York?" I asked, trying to sound merely politely interested.

"At least until June," he replied. "Perhaps a bit longer. And if Mr. Johnston is in favor of the proposal I have made to him, I shall go back to Boston to wind things up there, and then move here permanently."

He paused as the maid came in with the tray and remained silent after she left, watching me warm the pot with hot water before making the tea. Then he leaned forward suddenly and smiled at me.

"Now, tell me about your family. Are you, like me, an only child?"

I told him about my parents and Henry, and when I

explained Aggie's absence that evening he laughed, and said he'd had an aunt who had espoused the same cause.

"I used to worry when I was at Harvard that she'd appear and catch me in a pub with a stein of beer in my hand. My parents were embarrassed by her activities, thought she was making a spectacle of herself handing out leaflets on the street, and all that. I think they were relieved when she became housebound with rheumatism, and had to be satisfied with writing letters to the newspapers."

In the course of the evening I learned that he had graduated from Harvard Law School in 1884, and since that time had been employed in the legal office of the Boston Museum. Both his parents had died two years ago, he said, in an epidemic of typhoid fever that swept through Boston, so that he had nothing to keep him from moving to New York, and establishing himself in the museum that he thought would grow to be the most prestigious one in the country.

I asked him what kinds of legal problems occupied him, and was amazed to learn of the number of suits brought against forgers, crooked art dealers, and purveyors of stolen goods. I had never associated crime with a museum. We both chuckled, though, over the story of the old gentleman who became so enraged at the curator for refusing to buy a huge porcelain bowl he had brought in that he smashed the object to pieces on the marble floor, and then sued the museum for damages!

All in all, it was a delightful evening, and couldn't have had a better ending: just before he left, John said rather hesitantly that he had booked a table at Delmonico's for the following night, and would I think it presumptuous if he asked me to dine with him?

That was how it began—the *grand amour* of my life. For the rest of the spring of 1887 a week did not pass without my seeing John Townsend; on Saturdays and Sundays we explored the city together, from the Bowery up to the Bronx (he enjoyed the ride on the El as much as I did), and one glorious afternoon we walked across the Great Bridge to Brooklyn and back again.

There was a splendid restaurant in the Osborne, which I liked better than the more popular Delmonico's, and we dined there frequently, sometimes in the company of John's cousin, Stephen Peabody, but more often à deux. It was there one night in early June, at a secluded candlelit table, that he told me that the day we met he had deliberately followed me out of the museum, after watching me from a distance as I examined the paintings.

"I was almost grateful to that ragamuffin, Millicent, for giving me an excuse to speak to you," he said, reaching across the table and covering my hand with his. "And if you hadn't hurt your ankle, I'm sure I would have thought of some other way . . ."

"You were extremely bold, sir, but I am very glad you were," I said, smiling as I watched his eyes light up.

"And I'm bold enough to hope that you'll continue to be glad, my dear. Look at me, Millicent; I want very much to marry you, but I can't ask you yet, not until Mr. Johnston lets me know about the position at the Metropolitan—but tell me one thing—I have to know—is there . . ."

He broke off as the waiter came with our dessert.

"I have to know," he repeated, "if there is anyone else."

I assured him that I was not interested in anyone else, and then, so that he would not think I had never had a suitor, I told him how Papa had rejected Martin Grinnell's proposal, and how I'd been afraid he'd arrange a marriage between me and Mr. Bushwick. I thought John would be amused at my description of the latter, but instead he looked rather grim, and said something about arranged marriages being criminal.

"Oh, I wouldn't have stood for it," I said lightly. "I'd have run away. Maybe I'd have hidden in the museum, and you'd have found me there. Shall we stop in and look at the pictures together some Saturday? I'd love to see the Vermeer again."

★ ★ ★

I had not been paying much attention to Aggie's disapproval of what she called my "gallivanting," but the night John took me to see Ada Rehan in *The Taming of the Shrew* and to supper afterwards, I could not ignore her anger. How could I be so thoughtless, staying out until all hours of the night with someone we knew nothing about? What would the neighbors think if they saw me kissing a young man at the front door? Did I want to disgrace the family? And did I know that was how loose women acted?

"I shall speak to Henry," she said as I gathered up my skirts to mount the stairs, "and he will have that person investigated. For all we know, he may be a charlatan, an embezzler—he may be after our money . . ."

"He is *not* a charlatan!" I exclaimed, stamping my foot for emphasis. "He's a lawyer; he handles the legal affairs of the Boston Museum of Fine Arts, and will soon be employed by the Metropolitan. Besides, he has a private income."

Before she could say anything more I turned and hurried up to my room. Whether or not she spoke to Henry about John Townsend I never heard; in any case, the subject never came up again.

4

All that spring I had been like a creature upon whom a spell was cast; I was twenty-two years old and in love, an enchanted being, living in a world in which nothing could go wrong. As the season progressed, however, I could not put aside a certain amount of dread of the ineluctable approach of summer and the separation it would bring. John was scheduled to return to Boston at the end of June, and in July Aggie and I would depart, as usual, for Lake Mohonk, where we would stay at the Mountain View House.

I was afraid that my last evening with John would be a sad one, full of sighs and tears (at least on my part), but it did not turn out to be that way at all. He took me to the Park Avenue Hotel, a huge edifice which ran from Thirty-second to Thirty-third streets, where we dined on their famous verandah at a table near the railing with a splendid view of the gardens below in the spacious courtyard.

As soon as we were seated he told me jubilantly that his transfer to the Metropolitan Museum had come through that very day, and that he would take up his duties there early in September.

"I'll be on trial at first, dearest," he said, holding my eyes with his, "and if everything works out I'll be well established by the first of the year. The salary is good, and with what I inherited from my parents, I should be in a position to support you handsomely. Will you—?"

He broke off when he saw me nod; I thought he was going to lean across the table and kiss me, and he might have, if the waiter hadn't appeared at that moment and presented him with the wine list. And what delicious wine we had! A sauterne came with the fish, then a rich burgundy with the meat course, and later cognac with our coffee. I felt quite elegant sitting there with the tiny glass in my hand, wearing my best gown, a watered silk in a soft shade of rose with a bit of chiffon trimming at the low-cut neckline and on the shoulders. I had seen heads turn as we were being shown to our table, but whether the admiring glances were for me or for John, I could not tell. He was looking particularly handsome that night, in his immaculate white dress shirt and waistcoat and dark evening suit.

I had thought that after our meal we might join the couples who were strolling around the fountain in the courtyard, at the far end of which a Hungarian band played throughout the evening, but John had something else in mind.

"It's a perfect night for a ride through the park, darling—look at the moon," he said, signaling to the liveried doorman to call a hansom cab. "And if you feel cold in that light wrap I'll put my jacket around you."

He put his arm around me instead, and as the horse clopped slowly along the tree-lined drives, I leaned against him, wondering if I would ever again be so happy. We did not talk much; we'd made our plans during dinner. If all went well, we'd announce our engagement at Christmas, be married in March or April, and live happily ever after. No, except for whispered endearments, we did not talk, but I remember his murmuring that I smelled like flowers, and asking what scent I wore. When I told him it was Guerlain's *Fougère Royale* he laughed and asked me to say it in English.

"Royal Fern," I answered, "but don't you think it sounds much more elegant in French?"

"Either way, it smells good," he said, putting his hand under my chin and raising my face to his. He kissed me lingeringly, and then, as his ardor intensified, I felt my whole body responding in almost agonizing delight. My reaction was not lost on him, for when he kissed me good-bye in the dim light of our vestibule, he did it gently, holding my face in both his hands before he spoke.

"It will be even more wonderful in the future, my dearest," he said softly. "Believe me." He folded me in his arms one last time, then turned and hurried down the stone steps.

5

In order to prevent the next two months from stretching out interminably, I made a deliberate effort to fill each day with activities that would keep my mind occupied and also tire me physically. I wanted to be able to sleep soundly at night, not lie awake longing for John.

Spending the day, or even part of it, in a rocking chair on the verandah of the Mountain View House would have driven me crazy, although plenty of women, Aggie among them, seemed to be content to rock the hours away. I can't imagine how they stood it, especially since there were so many other things to do. Since we had spent several vacations at Lake Mohonk with Papa and Mama when we were growing up, I was fairly familiar with the place. In earlier years I loved the nature walks organized by Mr. Smiley, one of the owners, who warned us at the beginning of each outing not to stray away from the group.

"These woods are dense," he would say in his kind, deep voice, "and you could easily lose your way a couple of feet away from the path. One young lady did just that, and became so confused and frightened that she screamed for help. As it turned out, when we found her she was less than a hundred yards from the hotel. So be warned."

I don't know how many times I heard that admonition, and although I no longer went on the conducted walks, I kept it in mind, and stuck to the familiar Lake Shore Road, or the

Undercliff Path, which ran around the lake and offered a series of breathtaking views.

On hot summer afternoons I needed no encouragement to bathe in the clear blue lake water, although I despised the ridiculous costumes women were expected to wear at that time. Those long-sleeved bathing dresses were generally made of twilled flannel, nipped in at the waist, and falling below the knees. Underneath the gored skirt we wore baggy-looking drawers that ended in elasticized bands at midcalf, and under *them* long black stockings. A straw hat completed this unbecoming outfit, effectively preventing the bather from doing more than submerging herself gently up to her neck, or bouncing up and down decorously while holding the hand of a friend.

Children were more fortunate: they were allowed to wear simple one-piece garments, not attractive, but not bulky, and permitting much more freedom in the water than their elders could enjoy. One year, when I was about ten or eleven, Papa allowed Aggie and me to take swimming instruction. The young man who taught us was an athletic coach at nearby Haverford College—I suppose he supplemented his income by working at the hotel for the summer—and we all loved him. He taught us to do a good deal more than how to bounce up and down, and in time I became a fairly competent swimmer, straw hat and all.

Thus the long walks and the swimming took care of my physical needs, while the works of Mrs. Gaskell and the Brontë sisters gave me the mental stimulation I wanted. I remember taking a copy of *Cranford* to one of the little gazebos that overlooked the lake and losing myself for a couple of hours in the author's ironic account of life in a small English village. I saved *Wuthering Heights* for rainy days; somehow that seemed appropriate.

I do not mean to imply that I stayed by myself for the whole summer; there were picnics, horse and buggy rides, and boating parties in the flat-bottomed rowboats that belonged to the hotel. The resort itself was owned and run by a Quaker family, so that although plenty of amusement was provided for the guests, there were some restrictions: no intoxicating beverages were permitted on the premises (much to Aggie's satisfaction), no gambling was allowed, guests were urged to attend the morning prayer service held each day in the parlor, and daily visitors were discouraged from arriving on the Sabbath.

When I wrote to John telling him about these rules he replied that he approved of them in principle, but that if he were a guest he'd skip the prayer service, and find some way of having a glass of wine with his dinner. But that was only part of his letter; the rest of it, like so many of his, was devoted to his love for me and to the life we would lead together. He sounded as anxious as I felt to get on with that life.

To my surprise, Aggie had a telephone installed in the front hall immediately after our return to the city in early September.

"It will save money in the end, Millie," she said, as if apologizing for her extravagance. "You'll see; I won't need to dispatch notes by messenger, and it will cut down on postage stamps, too. Of course, it would have been more convenient for me to have it on my desk, but the telephone man refused to run the wires that far into the house. I can't imagine why; Henry's telephone is in his study in the rear of the building."

She made it clear that the instrument was to be used for "business" purposes only, or in case of an emergency, a warning to me, I suppose, not to think I could hold long conversations with John. He laughed when I told him about it, and said that after we were married I should have a telephone in every room if I so desired. He intended to have one installed in the apartment he had rented for himself across the hall from Stephen Peabody's at the Osborne.

"They're sizable rooms, dearest," he said, "and should accommodate us comfortably until we decide on a permanent place." He went on to tell me that he had made a point of seeing Henry, and apprising him of our plans.

"I know I don't need his permission to marry you, Millicent, but it seemed the right thing to do. I want to be sure your family knows that my intentions are honorable, that everything is aboveboard."

Apparently Henry made no objection—I would have paid no attention if he had—and over the course of the autumn we were invited to dine at the Forty-ninth Street house a number of times. Of course, Aggie was included on these occasions; she would have been furious if she ever found out that John and I had been entertained there without her. While she never said she approved of John, I could see her responding favorably to the little attentions he paid her, always addressing her as Miss Cobb, holding a chair for her, or presenting her with flowers or a box of chocolates when he came to our house for dinner. I thought she might be beginning to like him, as much as she could like anyone, and was delighted that there was no friction between them. That would have made things difficult.

As she and I did not discuss John or our plans for the future I assumed she had no interest in them, but I was wrong there: she was, as it turned out, quite interested, and had been making plans of her own.

On Christmas Eve I was up on a stepladder, hanging Mama's old-fashioned tinseled ornaments on the tree that had been set up in a corner of the parlor, when John was shown in. Aggie had gone upstairs to look for the angel we always put on the topmost branch, and when he saw that I was alone he strode across the room, lifted me down from the ladder, and held me close while he covered my face with kisses. Then, without speaking, he took a small box from his pocket and opened it carefully. A moment later he caught hold of my hand and slipped the diamond ring on my finger.

"Is it all right? Do you like it?" he asked anxiously. "If not, I can exchange—"

"Oh, John! I love it! It's the most beautiful . . ." I stopped when I saw Aggie coming in with the angel.

"Well," she said briskly after glancing at the ring. "Now that your engagement is official, we had better start making arrangements. After you're married you can move into Mama's old room, Millie, and John can have Papa's dressing room. Here, sir, you're tall enough to put this angel in place."

I could tell by his expression that John was as astonished as I was, but he said nothing until he had positioned the angel on the tree. Then he turned and faced Aggie.

"Thank you for your offer, Miss Cobb," he said. "It is most kind of you, but I have taken a suitable flat at the Osborne, and Millicent and I intend to live there until we decide on a house of our own." He spoke with such authority that Aggie let the matter rest, except to say that we could save a considerable amount of money by accepting her suggestion.

I was delighted at the thought of living in the bright, cheerful rooms at the Osborne, which John had described to me in detail, and when he took me to see my future home one rainy day late in February I was not disappointed. The Osborne was perhaps not as grand as the Dakota up on Central Park West, but it was newer, and equipped with all sorts of conveniences. Each apartment was provided with electric lights and steam heat, two luxuries I had never known, and in the public areas there were shops, a doctor's office, and of course, the restaurant where I had dined several times.

John's apartment was tastefully furnished, and from his seventh-floor windows (decorated with Tiffany glass) one could see almost to the southern tip of Manhattan. I was so enraptured with the appointments, the deep carpet, the softly glowing lamps, the wood-burning fireplace, and the comfort of the down cushions on the sofa that when it was time to go to dinner I did not want to leave. When I said as much to John he smiled, and after asking me what I would like to eat, telephoned down to the restaurant and ordered our meal to be sent up.

Of course I knew that I should not be dining unchaperoned with a man in his rooms, but I was too happy to care or to worry. Nor did I give a thought to propriety when, after the waiter had cleared away the plates and wineglasses, John came up to where I stood looking out the window, took me in his arms, and pressed my body against his.

For the next few weeks I was caught up in the special excitement that an approaching wedding engenders; we had decided to be married on the first Saturday in April, in a morning ceremony at Grace Episcopal Church, and Henry had volunteered to give the wedding luncheon at the fashionable Buckingham Hotel across the street from Saint Patrick's Cathedral. After that, John and I would leave for our honeymoon at the Chalfonte in Atlantic City.

Aggie, who hadn't bought any new clothes for ages, ordered an expensive dress for the event, a lovely lavender peau de soie, as well as a wide-brimmed light straw hat, trimmed with silk violets. She was to be my maid of honor, and I think she wanted to make an impression on Stephen Peabody, John's best man.

I hadn't intended to visit John's rooms a second time—I hadn't dared, although he suggested it more than once. But on Sunday evening, the eleventh of March (how well I remember that date!), when we were caught in a heavy downpour on upper Fifth Avenue he bundled me into a cab and instructed the driver to take us to the Osborne. He had bought a present for me, he said, and forgotten to bring it with him.

"We'll have a light meal sent up, dearest, and then I'll take you home. Maybe the storm will have let up by then," he said when we were warming ourselves in front of the fire. "And here's your present, Millicent. The moment I saw it in Tiffany's window I knew it was meant for you."

He watched as I opened the little robin's-egg blue box carefully and took out a dear little cut-glass perfume bottle.

"I thought you could keep your *Fougère Royale* in it—did I say it right?" he said, and smiled happily when I hugged him.

I cannot, or will not, describe the details of the rest of that evening; I must keep that to myself, to remember and cherish when I feel low. Suffice it to say that for a while we forgot about the elements, about the entire outside world, and devoted ourselves to each other.

It wasn't late when he took me home, only about nine o'clock; how I wish I had stayed until midnight, or later, when the rain turned to sleet and the streets became impassable with the ice that coated them. If only I'd stayed all night—but Aggie would have put me out of the house for good—I never would have let John venture forth the next morning.

★　★　★

The blizzard that had started as rain before turning to sleet and then to snow was in full force when I awoke Monday morning, and continued to rage throughout the day, piling huge drifts against the houses, some of them as high as the top of the stoop. By noon we could not even see the opposite side of Tenth Street through the wind-driven, swirling flakes, some of which drifted into the house under the window sash.

Aggie and I huddled close to the gas logs in the parlor, wearing our warmest clothes, not talking very much, just listening to the howling, destructive wind. The maids, gathered around the coal range in the kitchen, were probably more comfortable than we were, but it never occurred to us to join them.

The storm kept up all night and all day Tuesday before showing signs of abating, and it was not until Wednesday that we saw life stirring outdoors. A few householders were trying to clear paths to their front doors, which meant that sooner or later poor boys would come by and ask to shovel our steps. When I saw a horse-drawn sleigh pass I was sure that John would come as soon as he could; the telephone had been out of order since Monday morning, so I hadn't heard from him after he left me on Sunday night, and I knew he'd be concerned.

It was Stephen Peabody, however, who arrived in one of the sleighs late Wednesday afternoon, with the news that John's frozen body had been found in a snowdrift on Fifth Avenue two blocks from the museum.

"He must have tried to walk to work, Miss Millicent," Stephen said. "He often did, you know, in good weather. If it rained, he took the stage up to Eighty-second Street, but of course that wasn't running on Monday. He almost made it, too . . ."

I couldn't speak, I couldn't think; my mind seemed to be standing still, waiting, waiting—for what? for whom?

I don't know how long we sat in silence—maybe a few minutes, maybe half an hour—when Stephen put his hand in his pocket and drew out John's gold watch and chain. He handed it to me, saying that he thought I might like to have it, and then left me alone in a world that had fallen apart.

6

I have heard about people being driven mad with grief, and after John's death I think I might have welcomed madness—living in a world that had no connection with reality—if I hadn't known I was carrying his child. That the baby would be illegitimate, a bastard, did not concern me; he would be John's third and final gift to me, the other two being the diamond ring and the little bottle for my *Fougère Royale*. The watch I considered a memento, not a gift . . .

By the beginning of June, when my clothes started to feel uncomfortable, I realized that my condition could not long remain hidden. I said nothing to Aggie, but made an appointment to see Henry privately in his office. I intended to ask him to make arrangements for me to go to some secluded place where I could await the birth, after which I would return home and bring the baby up as an adopted child, the offspring of a fictitious cousin, say, who died of childbed fever.

I thought this was a perfectly reasonable plan, but Henry, when he recovered from the shock of my announcement, rejected it at once.

"Don't be ridiculous, Millie," he said with a dismissive wave of his hand. "It's too thin a story. People would see right through it. And what would you ever tell the child about his father? His ancestry? At some point in his life he'll want to know. Would you make up an entire genealogy for him?"

31

"What would you suggest then, Henry? Wait, before you answer, please understand one thing: I will not put the baby up for adoption, or leave it at the Foundling Hospital."

"Let me think about it, Millie," he said slowly. "I need time. It's a bit of a shocker, you know. But don't worry; I'll think of something. Have you told Aggie?"

"No, not yet."

"She'll have to know, of course, but let's wait until we decide what to do. Go home now, and I'll be in touch with you as soon as I've made up my mind. I must talk to Maria."

I was grateful to him, not only for taking charge of the situation, but also for refraining from lecturing me, calling me a fallen woman, a wanton, or a harlot, names Aggie applied to me later on. I would not have been so complacent, though, had I known then what he probably already had in mind.

Two days later I received a note from Maria inviting me to tea on Saturday afternoon.

"Don't bring Agatha," she wrote. "Tell her you're going shopping. This does not concern her."

I didn't have to tell Aggie anything; she left the house right after lunch, saying she was going to hear Frances Willard speak, and then going to a meeting afterwards. She did not ask me how I would occupy myself, but then she seldom did.

Maria greeted me warmly when I arrived at the brownstone house, and said we'd have tea in Henry's study.

"It's a more cheerful room than the parlor at this time of day, Millie, and more private, too."

What followed was more a business meeting than a social occasion, with all three of us feeling ill at ease, constrained. Henry sat at his large desk, with Maria at his right behind the tea table, and I sank down on the small sofa that faced them both.

"I think you'll agree with the proposal Maria and I are about to make, Millie," Henry said after the parlor maid had left, closing the door behind her. "We feel it's the best solution to an extremely serious problem. Now, bear with me . . ."

The plan he outlined was so far removed from anything I had imagined that I sat in stunned silence until he finished speaking. I cannot recall Henry's exact words, but the gist of what he said is as follows: As I knew, he and Maria had no children, and the doctors thought it unlikely that they would ever have any, which was the one disappointment of their married life. Therefore, Maria and I were to go away together; it would be given out that Maria was pregnant, and since it was known that her health had never been robust, no one would question the statement that her physician had advised her to spend the remainder of her pregnancy away from New York, someplace where the atmosphere was more restful and the air purer. Since Henry could not afford to be away from his business for an extended period, and since she did not want to be alone, I would volunteer to accompany her and remain with her until after the birth of the child. Then, upon our return to the city, the child would be brought up as their own.

"We've wanted children for so long, Millie," Maria said, breaking the silence that followed Henry's speech. "And you can be sure he'll have the best of everything, the very best."

"But will he not know I am his mother?" I asked.

"Not ever," Henry said firmly. "You must promise not to tell him. The only people who will be aware that the child is not mine will be the three of us and Aggie—I don't see how we can prevent her knowing. Don't worry; I'll see to it that her lips are sealed. There must be not even the slightest hint of the truth; you know what damage that would do to all of us."

"Of course you'll see the child, Millie," Maria said gently.

"On stated occasions," Henry said quickly. "His care, his

33

education, his entire welfare, will be up to Maria and me as his parents."

That, I think, was the moment at which I began to hate my brother. I said nothing, though; I waited to see what else was expected of me.

"Well, Millie," Henry said, not meeting my eyes, "what do you say? Do you agree with this proposal? If not, I shall wash my hands of the whole affair. But remember this: if you insist on keeping the child, you will never be able to hold your head up in New York again. And even if you run to the ends of the earth with him, he will still have no father, and you will be suspect for the rest of your life, no matter what lies you tell."

"I always knew you could drive a hard bargain to get what you wanted, Henry," I said as calmly as I could, "but I didn't think you'd use that talent against a member of your own family."

He made no reply, and after a moment I stood up to take my leave.

"But, Millie, what—" Maria began.

"I'll let you know my decision in a day or two," I said, turning away from them.

"Be careful, Millie dear," Maria said as she saw me to the door. "Are you feeling all right? Don't overdo. Let me send for a cab for you. We don't want anything to happen to this baby of ours."

Not ours, I thought bitterly. The baby is mine, John's and mine, and I have no intention of relinquishing him.

That night, and all day Sunday, I wracked my brain for an alternative to Henry's plan, searching for a way to keep my child with me without jeopardizing his future. New York society was fiercely intolerant of unwed mothers then, and for all I know, it still is, but I thought I could weather that.

What I could not tolerate was the thought of all the doors that would be closed to my child once he was labeled a bastard. And if I should have a girl, what chance would she have of happiness?

I went to bed in tears that night, and the next day, Monday, I reluctantly wrote to Henry saying I had no choice but to accept his proposal. He answered me almost immediately, congratulating me on doing the "sensible" thing, but his note also contained a threat. If, at any time, I revealed the truth about the baby, he would be forced to take strong measures. "By strong measures, Millie," he wrote, "I mean just that: I would have you declared insane, and committed to an asylum. And I have the power to do it. You will no doubt remember that Papa was ready at one time to have Aggie put away, and he could have done it easily if he hadn't been so softhearted. But I am not Papa, and if you breathe a word of this transaction, I will not hesitate to have you institutionalized for the rest of your life. Do not make the mistake of underestimating me."

I was so angry that I tore the letter into shreds before storming into his office and telling him what I thought of him. It did no good, though: a week later Maria and I left New York for a private facility in the Berkshires, on the outskirts of Stockbridge, the kind of place where no questions were asked.

7

The months I spent with Maria in that wooded, isolated part of Massachusetts passed all too quickly for me. I cherished each day that I kept my baby to myself, and tried not to let my mind dwell on the time he would be taken from me. Maria, on the other hand, found time lagging, and when I realized how bored she was without the bustle and activity of her city life I made an effort to provide some kind of entertainment for her. Thus, in spite of my condition, our roles were reversed; I became the companion, the planner of the day's schedule, the one in charge, you might say, solicitous of her comfort, instead of her catering to me.

Aside from taking little walks in the surrounding area, reading, or knitting small sacques and booties as we sat in the shade of the giant oaks that bordered the lawn, there was not very much for us to do, and at times I was hard put to find some relief for Maria from the monotony of our days. Fortunately her correspondence was heavy; she kept her friends in New York informed of the progress of her impending motherhood, and wrote long letters in connection with the preparation of the night nursery. This, she told me, would be in the spare room on the fourth floor, while one of the brighter rooms in the rear of the house would serve for daytime use. She would see to the furnishing of the latter upon her return to the city.

By coincidence, Maria and I had the same initials, M.C.,

which facilitated the impersonation of me as Mrs. Maria Cobb and her as Miss Millicent Cobb. I don't suppose it mattered very much; as I said, no troublesome questions were asked at that hideaway.

Although we were discreetly polite to the few other "guests" (all of whom were in an interesting condition), we, like them, kept to ourselves, limiting our relationship to a "Good Morning" or "Good Evening" when passing in the halls or on the stairs. I was interested to see that I was not the only one to have a companion; three other young women were accompanied by older ladies, their mothers, I presumed, and one lovely blue-eyed blonde had an officious-looking nurse in constant attendance. I remember thinking she was the only one among us who radiated happiness, and hoping that she would be returning to her lover. The others all seemed either grimly resigned or downright miserable. I do not know how I appeared to them.

When the brilliant New England foliage passed its prime and the weather turned cold, we were forced to spend more time indoors, and I was sure Maria would become restless. Instead, as my time drew closer, she became more and more engrossed in her plans, making lists of the people who were to receive birth announcements, deciding on a guest list for the christening party, and ordering great quantities of baby clothes. At first I was interested in her preparations, but when I realized that instead of *consulting* me, she was *announcing* her decisions to me, I felt passed over, left out.

My son was born early in December, and for two heavenly weeks I had him to myself, nursing him, holding him, adoring every inch of his tiny body, and treasuring each moment. When I told Maria I had named him John she nodded, but made no comment—which should have warned me . . .

Just before Christmas we returned to New York, little John to my brother's house, and I to my girlhood home, where I kept to my room for almost a month, sick with despair and the pain in my swollen, useless breasts. I was not invited to the christening party; I suppose they thought I might break down and spoil everything. Aggie went, though, and from her I learned that my son had been named William, in memory of Maria's father, William Walker Winslow.

8

Over the years that followed William's birth my anger at Maria and Henry smouldered, and as time went on, instead of forcing myself to become accustomed to the situation, I allowed my resentment of their possession of my son to build up. Oh, they never knew it; on those "stated occasions," birthdays, holidays, and such, when my presence was acceptable, I played my part, that of sweet, soft-spoken Aunt Millie, and in time convinced them that I was entirely satisfied with the arrangement.

It was not an easy role to maintain, and at first I was afraid that the overpowering yearning for my baby would cause me to snatch him from his cradle and carry him off. I went so far as to stroll through the park along the paths the nursemaids frequented with their young charges, hoping for a glimpse of him in his carriage. I stopped doing that, though, when I noticed one of the nannies watching me suspiciously, and resigned myself to seeing him only when it suited Henry and Maria.

This unsatisfactory state of affairs continued, virtually unchanged, until the winter of 1895, when Maria became so seriously ill with the influenza that she almost died. Henry was so beset with worry about her and fear that William would contract the disease that he sent the boy to Maria's sister, Mrs. Wallace Dodd. A few days later, however, he telephoned us, asking that Aggie and I take him until Maria was out of danger.

"Emily Dodd was quite willing to keep him," he said, "but one of her own children has come down with scarlet fever, and I won't have William exposed."

"We'll be happy to have him, Henry," I said, trying to keep the elation I felt out of my voice. "He can have your old room. Shall I pick him up at Mrs. Dodd's?"

"No need," Henry replied. "He's here at the office with me, and I'll bring him along shortly."

Aggie, not without a series of knowing looks at me, left William entirely in my care. I do not think she liked children very much; certainly she had never shown any interest in the ones we used to see at Lake Mohonk in the summer. I therefore had two unforgettable weeks with my son, escorting him to and from the private academy he attended, hearing his spelling words, supervising his meals, all the things a mother does. I was careful, though, not to hover over him, and to encourage him to entertain himself for part of the day at least.

He was delighted when I brought a box of Henry's old toy soldiers down from the attic, and devoted two or three rainy afternoons to noisy battles on the parlor floor. And I remember how pleased he was with the Parcheesi game I bought for him.

"Umm, you smell nice, Aunt Millie," he said, giving me a hug. "Not like Aunt Aggie." Then he practiced saying *Fougère Royale*, laughing as he did so, and that night he persuaded me to put a drop of the scent on his pajama coat.

In good weather we had little outings, a trip to the zoo, a ferryboat ride, or sometimes just a walk up to Gramercy Park. I find it difficult to imagine a better little companion than William was at the age of seven; his interest in everything that was going on reminded me of John's enthusiasm for the city when I first met him. He looked a little bit like his father, too, with the same eyes, the same ready smile, but there was also a resemblance to Henry in the shape of the face—perhaps that came from me.

It was while William was with us that a plan began to form in my mind. One evening after he had gone to bed, Aggie and I were talking about Maria, who was desperately ill at the time, and when Aggie said she wondered how Henry would manage without her, I hinted at a solution I knew would tantalize my sister.

"He'll need someone to run his household, Aggie," I said slowly, "and you're so good at that . . ."

I paused, knowing she'd jump at the chance of getting her hands on Henry's house, and when she spoke I knew she had taken the bait.

"I could certainly run it more efficiently than Maria does," she said. "She is entirely too extravagant, with four in help and all those wines at dinner."

"I don't think Henry would be willing to do without his wine, Aggie," I said mildly.

"Well, perhaps." Aggie looked thoughtful, as if she were already picturing herself the mistress of the handsome brownstone. "I will take Maria's room, Millie, and you may have one of the rooms on the fourth floor," she continued. "I shall suggest it to Henry when Maria—oh, well, time enough for that."

How susceptible she is, I thought, and how stupid! Yes, and greedy.

My plan to move into the same house as my son came to naught; Maria recovered, and William went back to Forty-ninth Street, taking the box of toy soldiers and the Parcheesi game with him. There was nothing for me to do but to bide my time until I saw another opportunity. It was years in coming; Maria was never very strong after the influenza, but she lived until the winter of 1908, when she succumbed to pneumonia. In spite of the elapsed time, however, the seed I had sown in Aggie's mind had taken root, and a short time after Maria's funeral, she approached Henry. I was not present when he refused her offer to preside over his household, nor was I too surprised, but she told me that he said he was quite satisfied with things as they were.

"He said that what with Aunt Carrie and Cousin Arthur there—why he took those two in, I can't imagine, and I don't think Maria was too happy about it—and William part of the time now, anyway, he said he had enough people around. There would still be room for us, though. Maria's room is still empty."

It was not empty for long; two years later Henry persuaded John Cunningham to let him marry his daughter, Sarah. Perhaps "forced" is a better word than "persuaded." No one knew better than I the lengths to which my brother would go to get what he wanted, and he evidently was determined to have Sarah Cunningham for his wife. I never would have known how brutally he went about it, though, if I had not been looking for a pencil.

I had arrived at the Forty-ninth Street house a bit early for dinner one Saturday night, and no one was about. Aggie had told me to go on by myself, since she might be delayed at a committee meeting, and apparently the others had not yet returned home or were upstairs dressing. I sat in the parlor for a few minutes, going over my shopping list (it was shortly before Christmas), and when I realized I'd forgotten my pencil I went down the hall to the study to find one.

As I entered the room, a sudden draft, probably caused by my opening the door, sent one of the papers on Henry's desk fluttering down onto the carpet. I could see that it was an unfinished letter in my brother's bold handwriting, and in a few seconds, without fully realizing what I was doing, I read what he had written. I placed the letter carefully on the desk, and deciding not to bother about a pencil, hurried back to the parlor, deeply shocked by what I had learned.

The exact wording of the letter escapes me now, but it was addressed to John Cunningham, Esquire, and stated that a painting Mr. Cunningham had sold to Mr. Roger Dubois, art dealer, as a Claude Monet had been declared a forgery. He (Henry, that is) was prepared to keep the matter from public knowledge by buying the painting from Mr. Dubois for the amount paid to Mr. Cunningham on one condition: that Mr. Cunningham would reconsider his rejection of Mr. Cobb's offer for Miss Cunningham's hand in marriage. Otherwise Mr. Cunningham could look forward to having charges brought against him . . .

As I said earlier, my brother would go to great lengths to get what he wanted. Obviously the letter was completed and delivered, and apparently Mr. Cunningham accepted the condition—perhaps he was afraid he'd go to prison if he didn't—because Sarah and Henry were married. I can see that Henry is mad about her: he almost idolizes her, but I've wondered if he isn't disappointed that so far she hasn't given him a son of his own. Aggie, as might be expected, is extremely critical of our new sister-in-law, and makes no effort to hide her feelings. I pretend to be fond of Sarah, but I really don't care much about her one way or the other. Perhaps I envy her, though; good fortune, which has passed me by, has not only showered her with this world's goods, but has given her a doting husband, and permitted her far more of my son's company than I have ever had.

I have often speculated on what she would do if I were to reveal to her the circumstances under which she was married, but of course, I wouldn't dare—Henry's retaliation is something I do not want to contemplate. Perhaps I would be wise to destroy this notebook; Aggie is such a snooper, and if she found it and showed it to Henry, there's no telling what he'd do, or what Sarah would do. I really can't think what attracted him to her—her youth and beauty, I suppose, certainly not her position in society; her family was anything but prominent in New York . . .

PART TWO

Sarah Cobb

1

It never occurred to me that I could have said no, that I could have refused to marry Henry Cobb, and I am sure that it never occurred to my father that I would not accede to his wishes. In 1910, in our little sector of New York society in Gramercy Park, parental authority was still highly respected, and arranged marriages were common enough to cause little or no comment. I am not sure, however, that Father was entirely happy about what he had done, because he sounded hesitant, almost apologetic, when he broke the news to me that he had accepted Mr. Cobb's offer for my hand.

"You see, my dear Sarah," he said slowly, after clearing his throat, "it is time I saw you settled. Your mother would have expected it of me. I am no longer young, and who can tell—but never mind that. Henry Cobb is a wealthy man; he'll make a good husband, and provide you with the luxuries I have not, of late, been able to afford. You'll like that, won't you? All the dresses and gewgaws you want?" He looked at me expectantly, almost pleadingly, as he waited for my response.

"But, Father, isn't he so much older . . ."

"Not *so* much older, my dear. Let us say he is mature, experienced in the ways of the world, which is more than I can say about young Bartlett and some of the other society fellows who've been calling on you. Now go and put on your prettiest frock; Mr. Cobb will be here this evening to speak to you. I shall not be present; I've not felt too well today, and wish to retire early. Will you have a glass of warm milk sent up to me in half an hour?"

I prefer not to remember my father as he was at dinner that night, nervous and ill at ease with me, but rather as he had been in earlier years, when he devoted so much of his time to my education and amusement. Since he had no particular profession—he used to say he "dabbled in the arts"—he was at home most of the time, limiting his social engagements to the evening hours after I was in bed. And how I loved the bedtime stories he would tell before he left! These were not the well-known ones in the standard collections of fairy tales, but delightful inventions of his own, more often than not illustrated with amusing little sketches in one of my copybooks.

Once in a while I would make up stories, describing the characters in detail. He would listen attentively, and when I came to the end he would present me with a leaf from his sketching pad covered with pictures of my heroes and heroines. I thought his drawings were magical, but apparently the publishers of children's books were not as enthusiastic, for few of Father's illustrations ever sold.

Gramercy Park was at that time, and to some extent still is, a quiet, conservative enclave in this bustling city, eminently suited to a man of my father's temperament. He had inherited the house we occupied, Number 17A, from a bachelor uncle (for whom he had been named) while still a young man, and brought my mother to it as a bride.

"I think the house was one reason she consented to marry me, Sarah," he said one mild autumn day as we were returning from a walk in the park. "She used to say she had always wanted to live on Gramercy Park, but had never expected to, and in such an appealing and well-appointed house, complete with a walled garden in the rear."

He paused, and glanced up approvingly at the sparkling windows and the neat boxes of late geraniums catching the last rays of the afternoon sun. I have seldom come across anyone as contented with his surroundings as my father was; I know that he felt it his duty to take me out of the city for at least part of the hot weather, to a modest resort at the seaside, or in the mountains, but I think that, left to himself, he would have stayed the year round on Gramercy Park, where he had everything he wanted, friends, shops, and Calvary Church conveniently at hand.

There were two schools nearby, also, reputable private academies, but I was not sent to either of them; Father thought me too frail, which was nonsense, but I was said to resemble my mother, who had died when I was a baby of what was called "a weak chest." He preferred to keep me close to him, and teach me himself, bringing in music teachers and French instructors from time to time. He also gave me unrestricted access to his library, and under his guidance I became far more familiar with the classics than most of my contemporaries. On winter nights we used to read aloud in front of the fire, chuckling with *Pickwick*, or despairing with *Oliver Twist*. Sometimes, though, I would read him a little story I had written during the day, purposely leaving it unfinished so that he would have to guess the outcome. He encouraged me to complete these little tales, patiently correcting my syntax as he talked, and later on, what began as a game on my part gradually developed into a more serious occupation.

I suppose it was my father's deep and sincere devotion to me that led me to trust his judgment in all things, from what colors suited me best ("Never wear green, Sarah. It is not right for your coloring.") to the choice of a husband. How immature I was, how innocent . . .

★ ★ ★

During the few hours between the time of my father's announcement of his plans for my future and the arrival of my suitor, I tried to recall everything I knew about Henry Cobb. It wasn't very much. I had been placed next to him (accidentally, I wonder?) at two or three dinner parties that winter, but had not taken any particular notice of his appearance. I suppose I thought of him as being one of the older generation. His age? I judged him to be about forty-five, which would make him twenty-five years my senior. (I later learned that he was fifty.) I remembered that he had a pleasant, cultivated voice, but I must have been more interested in whoever sat on my other side, for I could not for the life of me remember what we talked about.

I knew that he had called on my father a few months earlier, and that when he arrived he was carrying a rectangular package under his arm. I assumed it was a box of Whitman's chocolates, which were extremely popular at the time, and expected him to present it to me. My father, however, ushered Mr. Cobb, package and all, into his library almost at once. I sat reading by the parlor fire, thinking they would join me in a short time for a cup of tea and some Madeira cake, but when they had not emerged from the back room by eleven o'clock I went up to bed.

The next morning there was no sign of any chocolates, Whitman's or otherwise, and as my father seemed unusually quiet, I made no reference to the package. I did wonder about it, though.

I knew nothing about Mr. Cobb's occupation or his family, except that he was a widower. It did not seem very much to go on.

★ ★ ★

When he called that blustery night in February to ask me to do him the honor of becoming his wife, I was pleased to see that he was really quite a handsome man. He was fairly tall, and clean-shaven, with dark hair, and the brown eyes that fastened on my face were kind, gentle in their expression.

"You will be the mistress of a rather unusual household, my dear," he said after I had accepted his proposal and we were sitting opposite each other in the wing chairs that flanked the fireplace. "Besides myself, there is my son by my first marriage, William. He is not at home a great deal these days, having affairs of business that take him out of town frequently.

"Then there is my Aunt Carrie—Caroline—my mother's younger sister. She's elderly and frail, and keeps pretty much to herself. And at the moment Arthur Pierce is there; he's a distant cousin. I imagine his residence in my house is only temporary, just until his book is published."

The prospect of moving into such a large and well-established household was somewhat daunting, but I made an effort to hide any trepidation I felt by inquiring what kind of book Mr. Pierce was writing.

"A biography of Robert E. Lee," Mr. Cobb replied. "He's already written a couple of books and articles on the War Between the States, and I think he contemplates one on Grant. Arthur's an admirable fellow in many ways, but inclined to be a bit absentminded where business is concerned."

"And your own profession, Mr. Cobb?" I asked hesitantly.

Before answering, he smiled, and leaned forward to take one of my hands in his. "Would it be too much to ask you to call me Henry?" he asked. When I shook my head he relinquished my hand and sat back again. "I am a banker, Sarah. At least that is my main occupation. But I have other interests, railroading, shipping, and so on."

The details of the rest of our conversation that evening escape me now, but I remember that his manner was such that I felt quite at ease with him, not a bit in awe of his high position in the financial world. When he stood up, preparatory to taking his leave, I felt bold enough to put the question that had been on my mind ever since my conversation with my father.

"I hope you will not think me unduly curious, Mr. Cobb—I mean Henry—but I would like very much to know why you chose me to be your wife."

He smiled (I remember thinking how attractive he looked at that moment), and putting his hands on my shoulders, looked down into my eyes.

"Because I like your quiet beauty, Sarah Cunningham, and your calm outlook on life. And you really do ask the most sensible questions!"

With that, he kissed me lightly on the forehead and left. I stayed by the dying fire for almost an hour after he had gone, marveling at how swiftly events had moved in such a short time; only a few hours earlier I had had nothing weightier on my mind than tomorrow's order for the grocer, and now . . .

Well, I thought, I have done my father's bidding, as he knew I would. At the time it seemed the *only* thing to do, but now, looking back, I cannot help but wonder what my life would have been like had I defied him. Would some unimaginable horror have supplanted the one I later lived through— barely lived through? Or would I have had an uneventful, placid life of the sort that my father envisaged when he married me off?

I had no time to enjoy the excitement of assembling a trousseau, or even to have a wedding dress made, for less than a week after Henry Cobb's proposal, my father became seriously ill. It happened suddenly one afternoon when he and I were having our afternoon tea in the pleasant room overlooking the garden in the back of the house, the room he called his study, his studio, his atelier, his library, or his workshop, depending on his mood at the moment.

"Your mother loved that garden, Sarah," he said, getting up stiffly from his chair and going to the window. "There's still a rosebush out there that she planted, the pink one that climbs all over the wall every June. Dorothy Perkins, I think it is called—"

He broke off abruptly and grasped the edge of the library table with both hands as a spasm of pain wracked his body, and a moment later slid slowly to the floor.

My father lingered for six weeks after his collapse, heavily sedated with laudanum most of the time. Dr. Atwater, while kind and sympathetic, spared me none of the horrible details of the illness:

"The malignant growth that is killing him, my dear Sarah, is eating away at his organs, and the agony is at times intolerable. There may be periods of remission, but we can't be sure. The laudanum will help dull the pain, but it must be administered judiciously: three drops in water every four hours."

Without Henry Cobb's help, I do not know what I would have done. He more or less took charge, employing nurses, calling in doctors for consultations, sending over baskets of delicacies to tempt the failing appetite, and making a point of visiting at least once a day. He was there one Sunday when Father suddenly felt better and announced he would come down to dinner, and went out of his way to make the meal a pleasant one. I remember how he asked Father for his preference in imported wines, and promised to send over a supply, as if there were plenty of time . . .

On Monday morning Father had a relapse, and when the

pain subsided he asked me to bring Henry in to see him the moment he arrived; he had something to say to both of us.

I thought that perhaps he wanted to be sure that we knew he was to be buried next to my mother, or to give some special instructions about his funeral, but that was not the case at all. As soon as Henry and I were seated on either side of the old brass bed, he said he wanted us to be married at once, the following day. I could not have been more surprised, not only at the request itself, but also at the hoarse, querulous voice in which it was made, a voice that bore no resemblance to the carefully modulated one I had always known.

"If you wait until after I am gone," he rasped, "Sarah will go into mourning, and it will be a year before you can marry. Time enough for things to go wrong—you might change your mind, Sarah—and that could result in a scandal that would do irreparable harm to your good name. I want the marriage to take place immediately; then I'll know . . ."

I couldn't imagine how breaking an engagement would produce a scandal; I'd known girls who had handed back the diamond ring and been none the worse for it, but I felt it would be adding to his misery to argue with him at that point.

We were married Tuesday afternoon in Calvary Church (Henry knew the rector, otherwise it would have been impossible on such short notice), with only Henry's son, William, and my closest friend, Margaret Oliphant, as witnesses. Instead of a wedding reception of any kind, we had a quiet tea at Sherry's, and it was not until ten days later, after my father had been laid to rest, that Henry and I began to live as man and wife.

54

2

We did not have a honeymoon; Henry apologized for that, saying that later on, when he was better able to leave his business affairs, we would have a grand tour, all over Europe, if I so desired. So I simply went from one part of New York to another.

As Henry had said, the household of which I so suddenly became the mistress was an unusual one: William I had already met and liked, the reclusive Aunt Carrie and the absentminded Arthur Pierce I found pleasant enough, though rarely in evidence except at meals, but nothing had prepared me for the Misses Cobb, Henry's two unmarried sisters. True, they did not live in the Forty-ninth Street house, but they were there so much that at times I felt as if they did. They were both younger than Henry, and, as I was informed later, dependent on him for their livelihood. As soon as I met them it occurred to me that they might resent my position as Henry's wife, that they might think his marrying me would in some way affect them adversely.

They were there to greet me when Henry escorted me over his threshold for the first time. In the entrance hall a large mirror hung over the marble stand between the hat rack and little drawers for gloves, reflecting a good part of the front parlor. As I removed my wraps I caught a glimpse of them, looking for all the world as if they'd been posed for an old-fashioned daguerreotype. Miss Agatha Cobb, the older of the two, sat ramrod straight, her large, solid figure obviously severely corseted, and stared at me, rather rudely, I thought. The younger and slighter Miss Millicent had a far pleasanter expression, and smiled gently as she greeted me.

Henry told me later that he had not expected them to be there, or he would have prepared me for them. He also said he was delighted that I had not been intimidated by Agatha's forbidding appearance and brusque manner, but the truth is that I was not at all sure, at first, how to deal with her. It did not take me long, however, to realize that her interests lay in a managerial direction, and that nothing would have suited her more than to be in charge of her brother's household. No sooner had the introductions been completed than she announced it was time for tea, and marched across the room to the embroidered bellpull next to the portieres that framed the arched entrance to the parlor.

I was wondering how to assert myself, or whether to assert myself, when the matter was taken out of my hands.

"This is Mrs. Cobb, Nora," Henry said when a trim young parlormaid answered the bell. "She will be giving the orders from now on."

"Yes, sir," the girl replied, and turning to me, she dropped a curtsy. "How do you do, ma'am? Is it tea you'll be wanting?"

"Please, Nora," I replied. "Tea and hot buttered toast, if that can be managed."

"Oh, yes, ma'am. And Cook is just after taking some scones out of the oven . . ."

"And see if there's plum cake, my girl," Agatha interrupted.

"Oh, Aggie," murmured her sister, "you know—"

"Hush, Millie. A little plum cake never hurt anyone. And, if I may say so, you are in no position to tell me what to do."

A strange remark for one sister to make to another, I thought, fearing an argument. Millie just sighed, however, and looked down at her hands. I remember feeling sorry for her then, and wishing I could take her aside and converse quietly with her, but that was impossible. I was kept busy answering Agatha's questions about my family: how long had I lived on Gramercy Park, had I known so-and-so, was I related to the Murray Hill Cunninghams, and so on. When at last she consulted the watch that she wore pinned to her dress and said they must take their leave, Henry, who had been rather quiet during the tea party, stood up with such alacrity that Millie was startled and almost dropped the cup she was in the act of placing on the small table next to her.

"I can take just so much of Aggie," Henry said with a rueful smile when the door closed behind his sisters. "It's a case of a little bit going a long way. But come, my dear, you will want to see your room and settle in. Your trunk and cases arrived yesterday, and I imagine Nora has unpacked them."

I was curious about Agatha and Millicent, or rather about what influence they would have on this new phase of my life, but I was also anxious to inspect the household in which I would now be giving the orders. I therefore spent the next hour or so going through the rooms with Henry and meeting their occupants.

At first, after the coziness of the modest house on Gramercy Park (which my father left to me, and which Henry had advised me to put up for rent), the large brownstone near Fifth Avenue, with its high stoop, its marble entry hall, and expensive furnishings, seemed a bit overwhelming. There were five stories instead of the three to which I had been accustomed, and naturally many more rooms, laid out in what must have been a popular pattern with architects toward the end of the last century. The dining room and kitchen, both spacious rooms, were in the basement, the former overlooking the areaway and street, and the latter facing on a paved backyard (no garden here) surrounded by high fences on three sides.

The floor above contained the front parlor (where we had tea the day I arrived), which was separated by sliding doors from what was ordinarily a drawing room, but which Henry had converted into a large study-library for himself.

The third and fourth floors were given over to bedrooms, six in all, and the maids had the attics on the top floor to themselves. My own room, directly above the parlor, and by far the most lavishly furnished of the bedrooms, was connected to Henry's by a combination bath and dressing room. I was interested to see that I was to have a room of my own—well, I'd better explain:

I should say here that if it had not been for my dear friend, Margaret Oliphant, I would have had only the most rudimentary knowledge of the intimate details of married life. The Oliphants lived on the opposite side of Gramercy Park from us, in a larger and more elegant house, and led far more sophisticated lives than my father and I did. That did not interfere with my friendship with Margaret, however. I cannot remember a time when I did not know her; we used to say that our nursemaids introduced us to each other when we were infants being taken for airings on the quiet paths inside the iron railings of the park. We both have memories of playing together, sometimes just the two of us, sometimes with other children who lived on the Square, while our nurses or governesses chatted on a nearby bench.

As we grew older we were in and out of each other's houses, especially on stormy afternoons, and later on were frequently invited to the same dinner parties and well-chaperoned dances during the winter season. It was at one of these affairs, I think it was the New Year's ball at the Lewis Sanborn mansion the year we were eighteen, that Margaret met and fell helplessly in love with Richard Ealing, of the Tuxedo Park Ealings.

Their engagement was announced in the *Times* a few

months later, and when I showed the notice to my father, expecting him to be pleased, I was astonished at his reaction.

"I can't imagine what the Oliphants are thinking of," he said, putting the morning paper down on the breakfast table and staring thoughtfully out the window. "They ought to know what's being said about him: fast horses, fast company—the Ealing money has had to rescue him from a number of unsavory situations. Margaret's a fine girl, far too good for that young man."

"He seems quite charming," I ventured.

"I do not doubt that, my dear Sarah," he said quickly, "and I imagine it's that very charm that leads to trouble. No, no, she shouldn't be allowed—but it's not my concern. In any case, I am glad you've had nothing to do with him."

As it happened, Margaret was spared what might have been a disastrous marriage: Richard Ealing was killed that summer in a fall from his horse after a wild party somewhere near Tuxedo Park. Before that, however, he had initiated Margaret into what we referred to as "the facts of life," the details of which she passed on to me.

"You mean you really slept with him?" I asked when we were alone together one afternoon shortly after the accident. "And you let him—I don't see how—"

"You remember, Sarah," she interrupted, "how on several occasions Mr. and Mrs. Ealing entertained for Richard and me at Tuxedo, don't you? I wish your father had let you attend those parties—well, anyway, the house is simply enormous, and no one could ever keep track of where all the guests were. Richard's room was not too far from the one assigned to me, and he'd wait until late at night—oh, Sarah, it was so wonderful—of course it hurt a bit the first time, but after that—oh, Sarah, I was so in love with him, maybe I still am. Maybe I'll never get over him."

She sat with downcast eyes for a moment or two, and then shook her head. "At least I'm not pregnant," she said with a short laugh. "I suppose that's something to be thankful for."

Of course she did get over Richard in time, but that's another story. What I want to say here is that because of Margaret's confidences, I did not feel like a complete ignoramus when Henry came to my room that first night. This is not to imply that I was entirely at ease, for I certainly was not, but his lovemaking was so gentle and tender as he taught me what to do that before long any trepidation I felt disappeared.

3

I have never been quite sure whether Cook or I ran Henry's house in those days. Although she was apt to be impatient at times, if the maids dawdled, or if the butcher was late with the roast, Mrs. Murray was fundamentally a kind woman, and a person to be trusted. I think she was afraid, at first, that I would make impossible demands, or cause drastic changes to come about, but when she realized I had no such thing in mind she relaxed and became quite friendly.

I would go down to the kitchen each morning to confer with her about the day's menus, and by the end of the first week she was urging me to sit in the padded rocking chair next to the big coal range "to take the chill out of my bones" while we talked and drank strong Irish tea.

"That new iceman is the limit, Mrs. Cobb, that he is," she complained to me one morning. "Tracking in dirt and wet with his big boots. The old one I had trained to wipe his feet before he dared come into my kitchen, but he's been taken bad with the lumbago, poor man. And this one! He just smiles at me when I scold him, the bold rascal!"

"Would you like me to speak to him, Mrs. Murray?"

"Lord love ye, ma'am, no indeed. I'll teach him, I will."

I don't know what she said or did, but a week or so later I caught a glimpse of the young man carefully using the boot scraper at the areaway door.

Without Cook's help, it would have taken far longer for

61

me to familiarize myself with the workings of the household than it did. From her I learned that the first Mrs. Cobb had had a personal maid who demanded almost as much service as the mistress herself. I thought she was wondering why I did not have one, so I told her that Mr. Cobb said I could hire one if I liked, but that I did not feel the need of one. She looked relieved, and went on to tell me that Bridget and Nora were responsible for the upstairs chores, that certain rooms were "turned out" on certain days, that a laundress came three times a week, and that early every morning the former iceman's brother-in-law arrived to tend the furnace in the cellar and bring up coal for the kitchen range, and also to clear the snow from the stoop when necessary.

Understandably, Cook was an authority on the likes and dislikes of the members of the family as far as meals went.

"No use ordering a pork roast, ma'am," she said, shaking her head. "Only one to like it is Mr. Pierce. Better stick to beef, lamb, and chicken, with fish once a week. Very partial to my fish chowder, the master is. Now, Miss Carrie, she eats no more than a thimbleful, at the table, that is. She thinks no one sees it, but she'll slip things—biscuits and that—into her pockets and take them up to her room. The girls are forever finding crumbs in her bed. We'll be having mice up there next."

Henry's Aunt Carrie, a mere slip of a woman in her early seventies, was a consummate artist at self-effacement. She appeared promptly at meals, where, as Cook said, she ate very little, and she occasionally left the house to go to the lending library for the latest romantic novel, but most of her life seemed to be spent in her bedroom, which was directly above mine. When I asked Henry if she'd had a hard life he looked thoughtful for a moment before replying.

"As far as I know, Sarah," he said slowly, "she lived quite comfortably while her husband, Jim Curtis, was alive. He died about fifteen years ago, and apparently did not leave her well provided for. He'd only been gone a few years when she appeared on my doorstep in tears, saying all her money was gone and she had no place to live.

"Naturally I took her in. She looked so ill and miserable that I had Dr. Gillespie look at her. He said she was severely undernourished, almost on the verge of starvation, and prescribed a diet for her. We couldn't get it out of her when she'd last had any food. The next day I made inquiries at the building where she and Uncle Jim had rented a flat, and found it almost empty of furniture. The poor woman had been selling it, piece by piece, to pay the rent, and when there was nothing left except a bed and a few odds and ends, she came here. At times she seems a little scatterbrained, but then again, she can be pretty sharp. In any case, she's a harmless old soul. My mother was quite fond of her in the old days . . ." His voice drifted off. I imagined he was remembering the Aunt Carrie he'd known as a boy.

"She's as sweet as she can be, Henry," I said quickly, in case he thought I might have some objection to her. "And so shy. She just disappears into her room, as if she's afraid of the rest of us. When I asked her to take tea with me the other afternoon she became all flustered and darted upstairs."

"You mustn't worry about her, my dear. You'll win her over in time—you're so gentle with her. Now, enough of Aunt Carrie; it's time you turned your attention to me."

As I have already mentioned, Aunt Carrie's room was directly above mine, with the spare room (really no more than a hall bedroom) next to it. Cousin Arthur Pierce occupied one of the single bedrooms in the rear of the fourth floor, and William the other one when he was in town. All those rooms, including the large bathroom in the center of the building, opened off a long, dark hall, in which the gas fixture burned day and night. Agatha said over and over again that this was a disgraceful waste of money, but we all knew Aunt Carrie was afraid of stumbling in the dark, so it was kept on.

Like Aunt Carrie, Cousin Arthur made few demands on the household. A soft-spoken, scholarly-looking man of about forty, with graying hair and pale blue eyes, he left the house every morning for the Public Library down on Fifth Avenue and Forty-second Street, not returning until late in the afternoon. His equable disposition and dry sense of humor made conversation with him easy, and I enjoyed the rare occasions when he came home early enough for tea. At first I was puzzled that he was so reticent about his work, but Henry told me that authors were like that, unwilling to talk about the "work in progress," for fear it would go all wrong. Perhaps that is true, but after I accidentally came upon Cousin Arthur dozing over an open book on the table in front of him in the great Reading Room of the library, I began to wonder just how much work he was in fact doing.

William, the remaining occupant of the fourth floor, could hardly be considered a member of the household, since he was there so seldom, but when he did come home, the place was immediately filled with bustling activity and good cheer. Cook made a point of providing his favorite dishes ("He's a great one for green apple pie, Mrs. Cobb"), Cousin Arthur and Henry vied for his attention, and even Aunt Carrie beamed at him across the dinner table. And I must say I delighted in his company.

After graduating from Columbia with a degree in engineering, he took a position with the Starret Brothers Construction Company, and spent the greater part of his time in their Chicago offices. He was as tall as Henry, but not as heavy, and in a way looked like his father, although his eyes were blue and his hair light brown as against Henry's darker coloring. He was only twenty-three when I first met him, but a mature twenty-three, and far more interesting than the other young men of that age I had known.

The fact that he had a stepmother younger than himself

seemed to amuse him, for which I was grateful; things might have been difficult had he resented me. As it was, he seemed to accept me without reservation, and gave every indication of being genuinely interested in what I had to say and in what I was reading. He was extremely well-read himself, and rather surprised, I thought, that I was familiar with so many of the authors he admired.

I remember one Saturday afternoon in particular—dear God, I have ample reason to remember it: William had been working in the New York office for a week, and was due to return to Chicago the next day. We were sitting in the parlor, waiting for Henry to come in for tea, and talking about Dickens.

"My father loved him," I said. "We used to read his favorite passages from *Pickwick* and *Great Expectations* or one of the others aloud after dinner."

"I keep going back to *Nickleby*," he said. "But then again—"

At that moment I heard the front doorbell, and my heart sank; when that bell rang at four o'clock on a Saturday afternoon (or any other day, for that matter), it meant that Henry's sisters were arriving—he would have used his key—and Agatha would carry on . . .

At that time I had been married for a little over a year, and probably should have been able to accept the frequent visits of the Misses Cobb with equanimity. I couldn't, though; more often than not Agatha's loudly voiced complaints and criticisms ("Why on earth did you choose bright red for those cushions, Sarah?") bothered me. The day William was there was no exception.

"You really should train that girl better, Sarah," she said as she sailed into the parlor. "She addressed Millie as Miss Cobb! Everyone knows that *I* am Miss Cobb, and that Millie is Miss Millicent. Why can't she remember that?"

"Oh, Aggie, you fluster the poor girl," Millie said softly.

I saw William grimace as he stood up to greet his aunts.

"She doesn't change, does she?" he whispered to me. No, I thought, nor will she ever; she'll go on and on, hinting broadly that I am not capable of running her brother's house properly. Why she couldn't be content with managing her own establishment, I could not imagine, especially since she had ample means with which to do so. Henry had explained the financial situation of his sisters to me shortly after we were married:

"When my father died, Sarah," he said, "he left his entire estate to me, the only son, with the stipulation that Millie and Aggie be allowed to continue to live in the family home down on Tenth Street until they married, and that they be given sufficient funds to enable them to carry on as they had in the past. As you might imagine, *I* got out of there as soon as I could; I'd had enough of Aggie by the time I was ten. Fortunately, I've been able to see that they have more than enough money to live comfortably, without a worry in the world. Aggie's hard to please, but Millie's no problem. In fact, she's been invaluable at times. I won't go so far as to say Aggie is unstable, but there were times when we were growing up when she'd fly into a rage over some trifle, and Millie was the one to calm her down, something neither of my parents could do."

"About Millie, Henry," I said when he paused. "Couldn't she have married? She must have had chances; she's so sweet, and such a pretty woman."

"I think there was someone once," Henry said vaguely, "but nothing ever came of it. Millie doesn't talk about it."

But I must get back to the afternoon that William was there, because it was then that Agatha so overstepped the bounds of propriety that Henry became angry. The tea party was not going well for Agatha at all; I could see that she resented the way William took Millie over to sit with him on the love seat, where they talked and laughed companionably, and that she was annoyed at Henry for some reason or other. To make matters worse, there was no plum cake that day;

Cook had sent up William's favorite jam tarts. We all knew she was displeased, but we were accustomed to seeing her sulk, and none of us was ready for the malicious remark her discomfiture caused her to make. She waited for a lull in the conversation before speaking.

"Do you really think, Henry," she asked in a voice loud enough for everyone to hear, "that it is seemly for Sarah to be seen strolling along, laughing and talking, arm in arm, with your son in Central Park?"

"Aggie!" thundered Henry, as William and I stared wide-eyed at him. I had never seen him so furious. "How dare you interfere with what my wife does? You will—"

"People will talk—" she began.

"Damn people!" Henry shouted, putting down his teacup and standing up. "You will apologize, Aggie, and then you will leave my house! This time you have gone too far!"

"My own brother," she muttered, "whose reputation and welfare I have at heart . . ."

"Aggie! Did you hear me?" Henry took a step toward her, looking so menacing that I was afraid he would strike her. "You will apologize at once to Sarah and William . . ."

"I'll do no such thing. Come, Millie. I'll not stand for this!"

She swept out of the room, her long bombazine skirt swishing across the carpet. Millie, undecided whether to follow her sister or not, looked so woebegone that William put his arm around her shoulders and said he'd see her home later.

"Yes, stay and dine with us, Millie," Henry said in his normal voice. "Give Aggie time to think things over."

In spite of the scene that took place in the parlor at teatime, dinner that night was an unusually lighthearted affair—reaction, I suppose. William amused us with stories about his landlady in Chicago, a timid soul perpetually worried about burglars, who made William check every lock on every door and window in the house at night. Cousin Arthur made us laugh with his sly imitation of a particularly stiff and prim librarian, and Henry, for some reason, was reminded of the time his father had mistaken the house next door for his own down on Tenth Street, and berated the startled maid who let him in for leaving a clothes basket in the hall. We laughed a good deal, and I think even Millie forgot about Agatha for a while.

We saw Millie occasionally during the rest of that spring, the spring of 1911; she was far too sensitive a person to call constantly, or to outstay her welcome. In June Henry and I sailed on the *Mauretania*, the Queen of the Atlantic, as she was known, for a second summer abroad, and devoted ourselves to each other. When we returned in September I found a brief note of apology from Agatha awaiting me, and although Henry permitted me to accept it, and we began seeing her again, I could not help but feel that she was biding her time—for something. To catch me out? I hope I didn't show it, but from that time on, I was more uncomfortable than ever in her presence.

4

It was during the winter of 1911–12 that I began to write seriously, first some stories for children based on the old ones my father had told me, and later short pieces on the history of Gramercy Park, most of which were published in minor periodicals. Henry was delighted with my efforts, and had a specially made desk fitted into a corner of his study for me so that I could work undisturbed while he was at the office. We were both amused at the reactions of the other members of the family to my literary efforts. William said he was not at all surprised, and teased me about producing the Great American Novel; Aunt Carrie, who by that time had lost some of her shyness with me, asked me to write a book like those of Mrs. Humphrey Ward; Cousin Arthur said that Ethel M. Dell and Mary Roberts Rinehart had better look to their laurels; Millie said she was proud of me; and Agatha, not surprisingly, commented that she had always thought scribbling was not a fit occupation for a gentlewoman.

"What about Mrs. Wharton, Aunt Aggie?" William asked slyly. "Is she not a lady of breeding?"

"I am not at all sure of that," Agatha snapped, turning her back on him and reaching for another cucumber sandwich. I looked at Millie, who rolled her eyes heavenward and sighed; we had all heard Agatha's unsparing condemnation of *The Age of Innocence*. "More tea, Agatha?" I asked quickly, to forestall a repetition of the book's faults.

I do not want to give the impression that our social life was limited to entertaining the family at tea, although goodness knows there was enough of that. Of course there were dinner and theater parties, even occasional skating parties on the lake near the Fifty-ninth Street entrance to the park, after which we would return to the house for an informal supper.

I suppose I was happy—although I think *contented* would be a better word—with the life I was leading, doing all the things Henry expected of me as a wife and hostess. Yes, it was all quite pleasant, and I was slow in realizing that something was missing . . .

It was a busy winter, and a fairly uneventful one, not at all like the one that followed. Then in June Henry moved us all out to Oyster Bay on the north shore of Long Island so that we'd be away from the city for the hot months.

I fell in love with the house he'd rented the moment I saw it; it was late afternoon as we approached it in a horse-drawn carriage that first day, and my immediate reaction was that here was a house that seemed to be almost a part of the countryside, so beautifully did it fit into its surroundings. A large, rambling structure of no particular architectural merit, it seemed to bask in the warm sun, with its front windows overlooking the blue waters of the bay beyond the private beach and boat dock. I caught a glimpse of a colorful garden on the south side, and closer to the verandah, which ran around three sides of the house, numerous roses were in full bloom.

When Henry heard my gasp of delight, he smiled and pressed my hand. "I thought it would please you, my dear. It seemed to me like the right setting for you."

I knew I'd be happy there, and I was, for the entire summer, and not just because of the beauty of the place.

Fortunately Agatha and Millie went to Lake Mohonk in August, and although the former had hinted rather broadly that their plans could be changed, Henry had not invited them to Oyster Bay.

"They could easily go to Mohonk for July as well," he said to me, "just as they did years ago—I suppose Aggie doesn't want to spend the money, though."

Cousin Arthur and Aunt Carrie were never any trouble, and William, who spent the last week in July and the first one in August with us, was a delight to have in the house. I was surprised that he chose to be with us for his vacation, since I knew he'd had invitations from families who summered in Newport and Bar Harbor, and I asked him if he did not find us dull by comparison.

"Not at all, Sarah," he said, stretching his long legs out in a lawn chair. "This is much more to my liking. More restful. All those formal parties bore me to death. I'd much rather loaf around here."

Henry, too, relished the informality of life in the country. He went in to the office two or three times a week, but invariably came home early in order to have time for a swim before dinner. He and William taught me to do a passable breaststroke, while teasing me about being encumbered by the skirts of my bathing dress. This was, without a doubt, the most unbecoming outfit I had ever worn, but modesty on the beach was de rigueur then, and I considered myself quite daring to dispense with the long black stockings and gloves that were still being worn by some of the older women.

Henry went out of his way to provide entertainment for us, especially during the two weeks of William's vacation: he had a croquet court set up on the side lawn, and made us all play; he took us sailing in a boat he rented from the nearby yacht club, and organized outings in the Model T Ford car he bought so that we would not be dependent on the village taxi.

I have a picture of us crowded into that old-fashioned and uncomfortable car. I think Nora or Bridget must have taken it. Henry is in the driver's seat, with both hands on the steering wheel, looking as important as the captain of a huge vessel. I am sitting next to him, wearing a long coat, a duster, and have tied a scarf over my hat to keep it from blowing off. Cousin Arthur is in the backseat with William and Aunt Carrie, all three of them well hatted and coated. If it were not for the flowering hydrangea bushes in the background, one would think we were starting out on a cold day in January instead of on a midsummer afternoon.

We are all wearing special goggles against the dust and wind—I remember how I hated the way they pressed on my nose—because unless it rained, we drove with the top down. And what a business it was to put that top up if we were caught in a shower! It took at least two people to unstrap it, pull it up, and fasten it to the heavy glass windshield. Then there were the isinglass rain curtains to be fitted and snapped into place. All of this took several minutes to accomplish, and we were generally fairly well soaked by the time we were on the road again.

Amazingly enough, no one ever complained, and the only time I saw Henry exasperated was when we had two tires punctured in one afternoon. Fortunately the second one occurred in the little town of Roslyn, where we had gone to do some shopping, and he was able to get help from the garage near the old Clock Tower.

That would have been enough for one day, but on the way home we nearly had an accident: Aunt Carrie had bought a kitten from a little boy ("It was only five cents, Sarah, and he said his mother would make him drown it if he didn't sell it"). She held it in her lap as we drove home, and I suppose everything would have been all right if she hadn't been jolted when we went over a bump in the road. She lost her grip on the kitten, which sprang off her lap and landed on the back of Henry's neck, causing him to swerve and almost collide with a horse-drawn hay wagon that was approaching from the opposite direction. No one said a word, but when we got home I noticed that Henry refused tea and poured himself a large whiskey.

We didn't have many automobile outings after that. I remember just one: we set out to see Sagamore Hill, the estate where ex-President Roosevelt was recovering from a gunshot wound. We never found it; we lost our way somewhere alone the line, and just meandered through the narrow dirt roads. Shortly after that, William left for Chicago, and since Henry found it necessary to commute to the city more frequently, the rest of us had to be content to stay on the premises—not that that was any hardship.

Aunt Carrie seemed to blossom that summer. She fluttered about, dividing her time between the kitten and her flower arranging. She asked me one morning if she could "do" the flowers for the table, and produced a remarkably lovely arrangement of larkspur, stock, and some feathery greens she found at the edge of the woods. From then on she spent hours in the garden, talking to herself—or to the flowers— before deciding which ones she would cut that day.

She made an appealing picture out there on a summer morning, a frail, slight figure in an old gray skirt and a faded blue shirtwaist. I don't know where she found the battered, wide-brimmed hat she wore to shield her face, or the elbow-length kid gloves (they were the kind one wore with a formal evening gown), nor did I ask. Somehow or other, the costume suited her; I'm sure my father would have loved to paint her as she stood between the rows of asters and snapdragons in the morning sunlight.

Cousin Arthur busied himself with his books and papers for a good part of the day, but I noticed he would put them away with alacrity if I suggested a swim. I think Henry had cautioned him to keep an eye on me in the water. I did enjoy the bathing; by the middle of August the water in the bay had warmed up delightfully, and it stayed that way even after we began to feel hints of autumn in the air.

"I hate to see this summer end," I said to Henry one evening toward the latter part of the month as we sat on the verandah watching the sunset. "It's been such a beautiful one."

"We might prolong it a bit," he said, taking my hand in his. "There's no reason why we can't stay on through September. As a matter of fact, my dear, you seem to be so very happy here that I've been thinking of buying this property, in which case we could spend six months of the year here instead of just the summer. We could even come out for winter weekends, if you'd like."

"Oh, Henry! That would be simply wonderful! I'd love it. Sometimes I think I'd like to live here forever," I said, drawing his face down to mine.

"We just might do that someday," he said softly, holding me close to him and gently stroking my body as we watched the light fail.

5

That fall, at Margaret Oliphant's suggestion, and with Henry's approval, I joined the Madison Club, a conservative women's organization whose members professed an interest in the arts, primarily literature and painting. I found I enjoyed the companionship of the women who met for various lectures and discussions in the attractively appointed rooms of the limestone house on Thirty-seventh Street, formerly the home of a wealthy downtown banker.

Margaret and I made a point of lunching together at least once a week in the formal dining room that overlooked what we called the "Statuary Court" in the rear of the building. The banker had evidently had a penchant for large sculptures of birds and animals, none of which, I later learned, was considered particularly good.

I was surprised that my old friend had not married, but hesitated to ask her why, afraid, I suppose, that perhaps she had not after all recovered from the Ealing affair. Then one day she brought the subject up as we sat over our coffee.

"I am the despair of my parents, Sarah," she said, toying with the fringe on the little lamp at the side of the table, "not only because I have refused Selby Warner and Herbert Thomaston, but because I've been seeing a young man they don't approve of; he's an artist, Ronald Pate. Of course, he's as poor as can be, and all they care about is money. They often hold you up to me as a good example. And my

75

sister-in-law, would you believe what she said to me the other day—'It's just as easy to love a rich man as a poor one, Margaret!' Can you imagine that? And it's all so silly, when I have plenty from the trust fund my grandmother left me."

"How did you meet this Ronald Pate?" I asked.

"At one of Mabel Dodge's evenings." Her eyes lighted up. "She has the most wonderful salon, Sarah. You will have to meet her; she's an extraordinary woman, with so many fascinating friends, and working so hard on the big exhibition that's being planned."

That was the first I'd heard of the now famous Armory Show that was to startle the Old Guard of New York society with the works of the Cubists and Postimpressionists. I was immediately interested, and asked Margaret to tell me more about Mrs. Dodge.

"She's like no one you've ever met, Sarah," she said enthusiastically. "She *inspires* people—artists, I mean—and no one quite knows how she does it. I've heard it said it was just her presence—anyway, I'd like to introduce you to her."

I didn't take her seriously, but one cold afternoon in mid-December she did escort me down to 23 Fifth Avenue to meet the lady. I remember how bundled up against the wind we were that day, and what a shock it was to go from the gray outdoors into the stark whiteness of Mrs. Dodge's rooms. Almost everything was white, the curtains, the rugs, the marble mantelpiece, even the huge sofa at one end of the room. I did not find the overall effect at all pleasing.

Our hostess greeted us dressed in some sort of flowing robe—you couldn't call it a dress or a gown—also white, and was, I thought, barely cordial when Margaret introduced me. I found out later that her preference was for male callers, and thought that perhaps she tolerated Margaret on account of the Oliphant money. For me she had no time at all, and I never again attended her salon, which was probably just as well, since a short time later there were tales of wild drinking and even peyote parties at 23 Fifth Avenue.

I did, however, see Mabel Dodge once more: William, who was in the New York office of Starret Brothers for a few weeks in February, took me to the Armory Show, which was held in the old building on Lexington Avenue and Twenty-fifth Street where the Sixty-ninth Regiment had its headquarters. Henry, who had read the newspaper reports of the exhibit, chuckled when I told him at breakfast where we planned to go that afternoon.

"Just don't tell Aggie you've been there, my dear, or the roof will come off," he warned.

I knew what he meant. Agatha would surely have read the newspaper accounts, some of which labeled the show lewd, immoral, and indecent, and she would certainly believe them. I, however, was more puzzled than shocked by some of the paintings; I could make no sense at all out of Duchamp's *Nude Descending a Staircase*, nor of Pablo Picasso's strange *Female Nude*, the two most controversial pictures in the exhibition. On the other hand, I loved Vincent van Gogh's vibrant colors, and the mellowness of Claude Monet's gardens. We paused a few moments in front of Edward Hopper's *Sailing*, and agreed that it was one of the finest paintings there.

"Reminds me of last summer on the Sound with you," William said, and as we turned away from the picture, I saw Mabel Dodge. She was standing with a group of men who were examining George Barnard's huge sculpture representing the return of the prodigal son. There was nothing striking about her that afternoon, dressed as she was in street clothes instead of the flowing white robe; in fact, she looked quite undistinguished, even dumpy. In spite of her drab appearance, however, the four or five men who clustered around her were most attentive, addressing their remarks to her rather than to one another. Perhaps there *was* something special about her presence, but if so, I failed to detect it. Later on I saw her name in the catalog William bought for me; she was listed as an honorary vice president of the American

Association of Painters and Sculptors, which title represented a reward, I suppose, for her sponsorship of the artisans.

William did not miss my interest in the group at the Barnard statue, and looked at me questioningly as we made our way toward the exit. I waited, though, until we were on our way home in the cab before I told him about my visit to the salon on lower Fifth Avenue.

"Mabel Dodge!" he exclaimed. "So that's who she is! They say she does a lot for painters and sculptors, but—"

"Yes, I know," I interrupted. "I've heard the stories about her, and I never would have let Margaret take me there if I'd been aware of them then. Can you imagine what Agatha would say if she knew her sister-in-law had called on Mrs. Dodge?"

"She'd make Pa divorce you," he said with a laugh, "and then I should have to carry you off to Chicago."

"That would only make things worse," I said. "She'd come tearing after us to rescue you from me. Oh, dear, we shouldn't be making fun of Agatha, William."

And at the time, I thought that was all there was to it, a little fun at Agatha's expense, but later on I was not so sure . . .

It had begun to snow lightly when we left the Armory, and by the time we reached Forty-ninth Street, the sidewalks were covered. William helped me out of the cab, and kept a firm grip on my arm as we climbed the stoop. Once we were inside the vestibule he released me, but not before giving me an affectionate hug.

"I must run up and change these wet shoes," I said as I took off my furs and put my muff and gloves alongside the catalog from the exhibition on the hall stand. "If you ring for tea, William, I'll be right down."

Had I not been a bit flustered, I doubt that I would have left the catalog there where Agatha would be sure to see it, but she was far from my thoughts just then.

* * *

I was awakened the next morning by the noise of the furnaceman's shovel as he scraped away at the snow on the stoop. The storm was over, but the sky was leaden, and the outlook from my bedroom windows uncharacteristically cheerless. The shades and curtains of the houses across the street were still closed, as if the occupants had taken a look at the uninviting weather and gone back to bed. I shivered, and after lighting the gas logs in my fireplace, dressed in front of them in the warmest clothes I had, an ankle-length woolen skirt, a long-sleeved shirtwaist, and a knitted jacket I had bought when we were in Scotland.

Only Henry and Aunt Carrie were at the breakfast table when I went down to the dining room, the latter well wrapped up in an assortment of shawls.

"William left a few minutes ago," Henry said as he saw me glance around at the empty places, "and Arthur . . ."

"Turned over for another forty winks," chirped Aunt Carrie. "Not a sound from his room."

Henry teased her gently about keeping tabs on the people on her floor, and encouraged her to tell us about the time Cousin Arthur almost frightened the life out of one of the maids by suddenly emerging from under his bed, where he'd been looking for a missing notebook.

"Oh, Sarah's heard that before, Henry," she said shyly, "but, my goodness, he did give the poor girl a fright. And really, it was fortunate that I was there and saw it all . . ."

"As I said, you do know what goes on up there, Aunt Carrie," Henry said as her voice trailed off. "Now I must be on my way. I'll telephone you, my dear, if I'm delayed at the office, but I'll try to be home early." He kissed me good-bye and started for the door, where he paused a moment. "Keep a good fire going in the study, Sarah, if you intend to work in there. It's well below freezing out, and it doesn't look as if the weather is going to improve."

After he left, Aunt Carrie and I sat quietly over our breakfast, reluctant to leave the warmth of the dining room for the chill of the stairs and halls. From time to time she warmed her hands on the china coffeepot Bridget had placed between us, and I pretended not to notice when she slipped a muffin into the little drawstring bag she sometimes brought to meals. She nodded and smiled when I picked up the newspaper Henry had left, and was in the act of pouring herself another cup of coffee when a sharp scream from the floor above shattered the silence that had settled on the dining room.

The front door was wide open when I reached the top of the stairs, and Nora was pointing wordlessly at the black-clad figure lying motionless at the bottom of the stoop.

6

Henry was not dead; unconscious and immobile, he lay in his own bedroom, which had taken on a funereal aspect with the drawn curtains and the hushed voices of those who tended him. William and I stayed with him constantly, except to go down for meals that neither of us wanted, and on the afternoon of the second day the doctors we had called in warned us to expect the worst.

"Besides severe concussion, Mrs. Cobb," Dr. Gillespie said, "there is a strong possibility of internal injuries which have not yet manifested themselves. The outlook, in my opinion, is not good, not good at all, and Dr. Sullivan here agrees with me. If Mr. Cobb were younger—"

"But Henry is not an old man," I interrupted. "He's only fifty-three . . ."

"My dear, I wish I could reassure you. Of course, there is a chance that he'll surprise us and pull out of it, but I am not sanguine about that. We will simply have to wait and see. Now, I want you to get some rest; with two nurses in attendance, there is no reason for you to sit up all night again. I'll leave some laudanum for you. Two drops—don't take more than that—in a glass of water should enable you to have a night's sleep. You look as if you need it."

I'll give some to Nora, I thought after the doctors had gone, the poor girl is haunted by what she saw.

"I couldn't sleep for thinkin' of the master, ma'am, lyin'

there all in a heap on the stone," she'd said to me that morning. "So dreadful it was . . ."

She had been dusting the windowsills in the parlor, and happened to glance up as Henry slipped on one of the icy patches the furnaceman had been unable to scrape off the steps. Unfortunately he fell from the very top of the stoop; according to Nora, his feet simply shot out from under him and he hurtled down the entire flight of steps.

William was a tower of strength during the days that followed the accident. He saw to it that the nurses had all the equipment and help they needed, he dealt with inquiries from Henry's business associates, and even managed to keep Agatha from hovering over the sickbed. I doubt that I would have been a match for her persistence. I certainly had no intention of eavesdropping when I emerged from Henry's room after the doctors' visit, but when I heard Agatha arguing with William down in the front hall, I paused at the top of the stairs.

"I'm sorry, Aunt Aggie," William was saying firmly, "but the doctor left explicit orders that Pa must not be disturbed."

"Disturbed?" Agatha snorted. "He's unconscious, isn't he? How can anyone disturb an unconscious man, I'd like to know? Sarah's in there, isn't she?"

"Sarah is his wife."

"And I am his sister, a blood relative. And the only reason John Cunningham let Sarah marry him was because Henry knew—"

"Aggie! Don't . . ." I heard Millie's distressed voice.

"Don't you tell me what to do, Miss Millicent! You know what I mean; you're the one who told me . . ."

"Aunt, it's getting late, and you'd better go," William said. "We will telephone you if there's any change, and tomorrow—"

"Tomorrow morning we'll be back here, William. We shall keep a vigil. My own brother . . ." She was still talking when the door closed behind the two sisters.

William was still standing at the foot of the stairs—he'd been barring Agatha's way, I suppose—when I went down, and I could tell from his expression that he knew I'd overheard the argument. He said nothing immediately, but put his arm around me and drew me into the parlor, where the curtains had been drawn and the lamps lighted. We moved close to the fire at the far end of the room, and before I could ask what Agatha had meant about my father, William said we needed something stronger than tea, and took a bottle of brandy from the lacquered cabinet behind the love seat.

"What did she mean, William?" I asked as he handed me a small glass. "What did Agatha mean when she said Henry knew something about my father?"

"I have no idea, Sarah, believe me. Aggie's inclined to imagine things, make things up, especially when she can't get her own way. She made some pretty bitter comments when Pa told her he intended to marry again."

"I know she resents me, William. She has from the beginning . . ."

"She would have resented anyone he married. You see, it's partly fear for her own livelihood, of being left without enough money. She saw what happened to Aunt Carrie."

"But Henry's so generous . . ."

"Yes, of course he is, to everyone. But he could leave it all to you; that's what worries Aggie. I think the main reason she wants to be at his bedside is so she can ask him about his will the moment he regains consciousness—if he does."

"Oh, dear—and she'll be back tomorrow, making a fuss. Can you stay, William? You don't have to go back to Chicago, do you?"

"No, not now. I've explained the situation to the office . . ."

"Oh, I *am* glad! I do need you here."

We had remained standing during this exchange, and when I turned away from the fire to look at him, he took the empty glass from my hand and placed it on the tea table.

"You haven't any idea how much I need you," he said softly, and a moment later his arms were around me and his lips were pressed on mine.

I did not go down to dinner that night; Nora brought me a light meal, and when she came to remove the tray, I gave her a glass of water with two drops of laudanum in it, with instructions to drink it when she went to bed. She looked at it dubiously, but when I said Dr. Gillespie had prescribed it for me to help me sleep, she nodded and thanked me.

I was reluctant to take the sleep-inducing drug myself; the very sight of it brought back memories of the countless doses of laudanum my father had been given during his last terrible weeks, and besides, I wanted a clear mind with which to review (or relive?) the moments in the parlor with William. I thought I could still feel his strong, young arms around me, still feel the passionate kisses he rained on my face, and suddenly I realized that without question, he had aroused me in a way Henry never had. I remember thinking that it was strange that I did not feel guilty, but I must have felt so to some degree, because I could not bring myself to go into Henry's room to make one last check on him that night. In any case, I knew that the nurse would call me if there was any change in his condition.

I put the little bottle of laudanum next to a glass of water on my bedside table, within easy reach in case sleep eluded me, and prepared for the night. As I half expected, I lay awake for a long time, staring at the dim glow in the fireplace, my thoughts in a jumble. I kept seeing William's face bending toward me, and then with a start I'd remember

Henry, lying helpless in the next room. I hadn't known until then that it was possible to feel both happy and miserable at the same time.

It was almost midnight when I found the courage to admit to myself that I was in love for the first time in my life—and with my husband's son. At that point I sat up in bed and mixed the draft that would enable me to sleep.

7

William was with his father when I went into the sickroom the next morning. He glanced up at me, shook his head to indicate that Henry's condition had not changed, and followed me out into the hall.

"I'll be downstairs in a few minutes," he said quietly. "The nurse needs help changing the bed linen."

He didn't touch me, but his eyes held mine until I broke away and hurried down to the dining room, where Cousin Arthur and Aunt Carrie were commenting on the weather. Sometime during the night it had begun to snow again, and from where I sat I could see that it was coming down steadily. Perhaps, I thought, this will deter Agatha . . .

I should have known better: a little after ten o'clock she and Millie arrived, prepared, I was sure, to spend the day.

"Aggie, I told you we shouldn't have come," Millie was saying as I went into the parlor. "Look at that snow! How on earth will we get home?" And she sneezed several times.

"Don't tell me you've caught another of your colds," Agatha said crossly. "Oh, Sarah, there you are. When can I see Henry?"

"We'll see what Dr. Gillespie says," I replied. "He'll be here sometime today. Millie, you're shivering! Shall I send for a hot drink for you? Sit over there near the fire."

"Oh, Aggie, why did you make me come?" Millie wailed. "Can't you see what an extra burden you put on Sarah?"

"Hush, Millie. My brother's life is more important than any burden. I shall speak to Gillespie the moment he comes . . ."

Millie sneezed again, and pulled her chair closer to the grate.

"I'll see about some lemon and honey for her," I said to Agatha. Would you care for some coffee and a biscuit?"

"By all means, Sarah. I'm chilled through. And see if she's made any hot bread."

"Oh, Aggie," Millie moaned, as I turned to ring for Nora, "why do you—oh, William dear, no, don't come near me; I seem to have taken cold."

I waited until Nora came up with a well-laden tray and then slipped out of the room.

As I stayed upstairs most of the day, either sitting at Henry's bedside or trying to rest in my own room, I do not know how the two sisters passed the long, seemingly endless hours. I suppose that with the exception of lunch down in the dining room, they spent their time in the parlor, Millie huddled over the fire, and Agatha sitting upright in what we called the bishop's chair because of the mitrelike carving on its back. From there she had an unobstructed view of the front hall and the lower part of the staircase, thus allowing the doctor no chance of avoiding her. She waited, however, in vain; the snowstorm increased in intensity as the day wore on, and no one was surprised when Dr. Gillespie telephoned at four o'clock and said he doubted he would be able to come until the next morning. He spoke to William, listened to the nurse's report, and gave whatever instructions were necessary.

By that time it was obvious that the sisters would have to stay overnight. Even if the snow stopped, which it showed no signs of doing, Millie was in no condition to go outdoors. When I went down to the parlor at teatime, she was leaning back in her chair with her eyes closed, looking exhausted. William and Cousin Arthur were standing at the window watching the swirling flakes, and Agatha was talking (to no one in particular) about the blizzard of '88 and the havoc it wrought. As soon as she saw me come in, she broke off in midsentence, and held up the catalog from the Armory Show, shaking it at me.

"I found this on the stand in the hall, Sarah. Do you mean to say you actually went to see those disgustingly immoral pictures? What if someone we knew saw you there? Have you no idea of propriety? Those lewd paintings . . ."

"Never mind about the paintings, Aunt," William intervened. "We have to decide where you and Aunt Millie are to sleep . . ."

"It's simple enough," Agatha said complacently. "Since Sarah will undoubtedly sit up with Henry, I shall sleep in her room—Nora can change the sheets—and Millie can have the spare room on the fourth floor. Of course, we'll need to be provided with nightwear . . ."

"The nurse will sit up with Pa," William said, rather loudly, I thought. "Sarah needs her rest. You may have my room, Aunt Aggie, and I will move down to the daybed in the study. Now, take Aunt Millie upstairs and settle her in the spare room; she looks all in."

To my surprise, Agatha obeyed him.

Dinner was a gloomy affair that night, and no one was inclined to linger over it. Afterwards, when I went into the study to make sure the daybed had been prepared for William, he followed me, closing the door behind him. For a moment we stood quite still, looking at each other, and then, without a word, I walked into his arms.

A short time later, maybe five minutes or so, the night nurse knocked on the door with the news that Henry had regained consciousness and was asking for us.

8

The days that followed Henry's return to consciousness were almost as trying as the ones we had just lived through. He was, naturally, weak from his illness, and like most active men in their prime, impatient with invalidism. William and I had all we could do to keep him from ignoring the doctor's strictures, and going down to the study to phone his office. I knew it would be only a matter of time before he overrode our objections. As soon as he was able to be up and out of bed for a few hours each day, he dismissed the nurses, saying they did him no good at all, that on the contrary, they made him nervous.

"Can't stand anyone hovering over me," he said crossly when William remonstrated with him. "Asking me how I feel every five minutes, and 'Do we want a drink of water?' when I have a full glass at my elbow. Simpletons!"

As his strength returned, he was able to sit up in the big chair near the window for longer and longer periods of time. I was careful not to hover over him, but I did for the most part stay within call, and made sure he took the various medicines Dr. Gillespie had ordered at the proper times. He liked me to have tea with him, and he also seemed to enjoy having me sit with him for a while at night after he was settled in bed. Sometimes William was there with us in the evening, but he didn't stay long; I think it made him uncomfortable to see Henry holding my hand and playing with my fingers.

"It's just as well you weren't at dinner tonight, Henry," I said to him one night after William had left. "I'm afraid you might have killed Aggie."

"What did she do? Cause Cook to give notice?" he asked with a smile.

"No, but I think it might have come to that if Cook had overheard her comments on the food: the soup lacked salt, the beef hadn't been aged enough, the vegetables were overdone, and was green apple pie the only dessert ever served in this house? Cook makes it for William, you know. Oh, and Henry—I had to laugh—remember how Aunt Carrie steals a muffin or a biscuit from the basket and slips it into her pocket?" He smiled again, and nodded to me to continue. "Well, Agatha caught her in the act, and glared at her so that poor Aunt Carrie became flustered, and handed the biscuit to Cousin Arthur, who took it and calmly put it in his pocket!"

"Good for Arthur," Henry said with a chuckle. "But tell me, my dear, aren't Aggie and Millie ever leaving? It can't be easy for you, having them on your hands day and night."

"I really can't say when they're going. Agatha went down to Tenth Street to fetch some clothing. But, Henry, Millie's been very ill; Dr. Gillespie said it was a bronchial infection. She's up and about now, though, so I imagine they'll be going soon."

"The sooner the better," he muttered. "I know what a damn nuisance Aggie can be. I have made it clear to her that she'll be well provided for should I predecease her, but she keeps pestering me for more information than I am prepared to give her. I finally had to tell her that if she didn't stop bothering me, I'd cut her out of my will altogether, and that's keeping her quiet—for the time being, at least."

I was tempted to ask him what Agatha had meant by saying that I was allowed to marry him only because he knew something about my father, but when he yawned and asked for his medicine, I let it go.

"Leave a glass of water where I can reach it, please, Sarah. I wake up in the night feeling thirsty. Must be all the damn stuff Gillespie makes me take."

By the time I filled his carafe with fresh water and poured out a glassful for him, he seemed to be asleep, so after adjusting the comforter at the foot of his bed, I turned out the lamp and left the room, closing the door quietly behind me.

When I stepped out into the dimly lighted hall, Millie, who was halfway up the stairs to the fourth floor, leaned over the banister and beckoned to me.

"I thought I'd retire early, Sarah dear," she whispered. "Aunt Carrie and Arthur have already gone up, and I can't stand any more of Aggie's complaining. You'd better go down and rescue William."

I had avoided being alone with William since the night Henry regained consciousness, and had tried desperately to keep my mind from dwelling on him, but when I saw the look in his eyes as I entered the parlor (fortunately his back was toward Agatha), my heart leapt.

"Sarah, will you ring for some warm milk to be sent up to my room?" Agatha made the request sound like a command. "It may settle my stomach. Something we had at dinner has disagreed with me, the meat, probably."

I saw William shake his head, and knew what he was thinking: in spite of her criticism of the food that night, Agatha had eaten heartily, two helpings of everything except the soup. I guess eating was one of her few pleasures, poor woman. I almost felt sorry for her at that point, and was about to follow her up to see that she had everything she needed when William caught hold of my arm.

"I'll be leaving for Chicago tomorrow, Sarah," he said, drawing me away from the arched entrance, "and I will not be coming back. I love you, my darling; you must know that by now—no, don't cry! Oh, God . . ."

He folded me in his arms, kissed me roughly on the lips,

and stood looking down at my face for a moment before turning away abruptly and leaving the room.

I waited until I heard him close the door to the study before turning off the lamps in the parlor and making my way upstairs through the now quiet house. Agatha was coming out of my room when I reached the floor above; not in the least abashed, she told me she'd been looking for some sal volatile.

"This whole business has upset me terribly, Sarah. I don't feel like myself at all. I intend to ask Gillespie for something to calm my nerves when he comes tomorrow. Isn't there some sal volatile someplace in this house?"

I found it for her (it was in plain view on one of the shelves in my bathroom) and stood in my doorway watching her as she trudged heavily up the stairs to the fourth floor. The thought of her rummaging through my things was not a pleasant one.

After I undressed I took the little bottle of laudanum from the drawer of my night table, and held it in my hand for a moment or two before replacing it. I hadn't liked the deep, drugged sleep it caused the only time I had taken it, and besides, I wanted to be up early enough to see William before he left. His departure this time seemed so very final.

As it happened, he did not leave. When he went into the sickroom to say good-bye to his father the next morning, Henry was dead.

9

Perhaps it was because Henry had recently been so close to death that I was not as aghast as I might otherwise have been when I looked down at the lifeless figure in the huge mahogany bed. This is not to say I was not shocked—I guess what I mean is that the blow had somehow been cushioned by what had happened earlier. And while I am not proud of it, I must admit that one of my first thoughts upon realizing that he was gone was that now he need never know . . .

"You should never have let the nurses go, Sarah," Agatha said when we were waiting for Dr. Gillespie to sign the death certificate. "If the night nurse had been there, this would not have happened. You should blame yourself."

"That will do, Aunt," William said sharply. "Pa dismissed the nurses himself. Sarah had nothing to do with it."

"Well, of course you'd defend her. Don't think I haven't noticed—" Agatha began, but a fierce look from William kept her from continuing. She was not, however, the only one to blame me for Henry's death, as subsequent events showed.

All of us, Aunt Carrie, Cousin Arthur, Henry's sisters, William, and I, remained in the parlor while the doctor was upstairs examining the body. I thought he would be down in a few minutes to tell us to make the funeral arrangements, which is what happened when my father died. I was surprised, therefore, when after about a quarter of an hour William and I were summoned up to Henry's room.

"Is there something we should do, Dr. Gillespie?" William asked.

"No, no," the doctor replied. "I just want to get a few facts straight. What medication did he take during the night, Mrs. Cobb?"

"As far as I know he took nothing after I left him."

"What time was that?"

"It must have been about half past nine, maybe a little bit later. We'd been chatting; he liked me to sit and talk with him after dinner until he felt like sleeping, so I stayed until he yawned and asked me to give him his medicine—"

"Which one?" the doctor asked sharply.

"Why, the red cough medicine there on the table. I gave him a spoonful, and he asked me to fill his water glass and leave it within reach. He said he thought the medicine made him wake up with a thirst during the night."

"It could have," the doctor said thoughtfully. "I purposely prescribed an elixir with a small amount of codeine in it to help him sleep through the night, but it certainly was not strong enough to kill him."

"What are you saying?" William sounded angry. "Are you insinuating . . ."

"I am insinuating nothing, Mr. Cobb," the doctor said before turning to me. "You say you filled his water glass, Mrs. Cobb; did he drink from it then?"

"No, he didn't. I went into the bathroom to fill the carafe, and by the time I had poured out a glassful for him, he had turned over on his side and seemed to be asleep. I straightened the comforter, and turned off the lamp, and then went downstairs."

"Apparently he woke up sometime during the night and

drank it all," William said, nodding his head toward the empty glass on the night table.

We were silent for a few moments, and then Dr. Gillespie spoke slowly:

"Your father may very well have died of natural causes, Mr. Cobb, but his pupils are miotic—that means small—and generally after death they are somewhat dilated. I feel that we should have the contents of the bottle of the cough medicine and the carafe analyzed."

"You mean he may have been drugged?" I gasped.

"At the moment I cannot eliminate the possibility, Mrs. Cobb. It is true that your husband sustained a severe shock to his system, and he did have a slight heart murmur, but he was making a good recovery, and I cannot explain his sudden death to my satisfaction. There will have to be an autopsy—"

At that moment the door burst open, and Agatha, who had evidently had her ear to it, exploded into the room, her face flushed and her eyes flashing. I was suddenly reminded of what Henry had told me about her childhood rages, and wondered if we were about to witness a recurrence.

"Miss Cobb, if you will just wait—" the doctor began.

"Wait, nothing! I have every right to know what is going on! If my brother had been drugged, I will see justice done! I know—"

"Miss Cobb!" The doctor raised his voice. "Nothing will be gained by histrionics. I shall see that the necessary procedure is followed. Now, I want everyone out of this room, the doors locked, and the keys given to me."

Henry's bedroom remained locked after his body had been taken to wherever they perform autopsies, and there was nothing to do but wait while the hours dragged by. That awful waiting and wondering! I do not like to remember it. I don't know how the others passed the time, but William and I spent the morning in the study. We decided not to put an obituary notice in the *Times* until we had a report from Dr. Gillespie, but we did notify Henry's partners and business associates. I was sitting at the little desk especially ordered for me, making a list of things to be done, and William was sorting papers at Henry's larger one, when Agatha came into the room and demanded to see the will.

"It's not here, Aunt," William said. "His attorney has it, and will bring it over tomorrow." She had to be content with that. After she had reluctantly left the room, William sighed and closed the folder he'd been examining.

"Never in my life have I found it so difficult to concentrate, Sarah," he said, rubbing his eyes. "I suppose it's the shock." He paused and stacked some papers in a neat pile. "Everything here seems to be in order, but there must be a mountain of stuff in the office, and then there are still the contents of the safe to be looked at, and I don't know the combination. I know the Lincoln letter is in there, but what else—"

"What safe, William? Where is it?" I asked.

"Up there, Sarah, behind that picture," he answered, nodding to a small painting I had never noticed. It was in a corner of the room, partly hidden by one of the window drapes. "It's not very large," he continued. "I don't suppose there's much in it."

"What a charming little scene!" I said, going over to look more closely at the painting. "Rather like one of Monet's gardens, with the roses against the wall, and the little path. I wonder whose it is; it's not signed—oh, it looks as if the signature has been painted over."

"It's probably something my mother picked up," William said, turning around to look at the painting. "She used to go around to the galleries; Pa never showed any interest in that kind of thing, although Roger Dubois, the art dealer, was one of his good friends. Perhaps he bought it from him because it was the right size to cover the opening of the safe."

At that point the telephone rang, and we learned from Dr. Gillespie that the autopsy would not be completed until the following day, and that we could expect the report sometime after noon.

"He wants us all to be here," William said after he had hung up the receiver. "As if anything would budge Aggie . . ."

He broke off abruptly and came across the room to where I was standing in front of the picture.

"There's something familiar about this painting, William," I said. "Did we see one like it at the Armory Show?"

"We may have," he said, but he was looking at me, not at the painting. He did not take me in his arms or kiss me, but stood looking down at me for a moment before catching hold of my hands.

"You realize that you're free now, darling, don't you? And you know I want—"

"I know," I whispered, "and I know I love you—"

He did kiss me then, and held me until I broke away.

"We can't—" I began.

"We can go to Chicago, darling, and be married there. No one will know us, so there won't be any talk about waiting a decent interval."

"We can't decide now, William. Wait until after the funeral."

"I will, if you promise me you'll have me," he said, and smiled down at me when I nodded.

In spite of the aura of death and uncertainty about the cause of death that pervaded the household, I felt strangely light-hearted for the rest of the day, and kept to my room for the better part of the afternoon for fear my inner happiness might be visible. I do not mean I was completely happy; I could not help feeling some pangs of conscience about loving so

98

desperately the son of the man who had loved and trusted me.

By common consent we all retired early that night, in fact, so early that I measured out two drops of laudanum so that I would be sure to sleep. For some reason, though, the drug had no effect, and I lay wide awake, wondering if I had become immune to it. For a while I heard Aunt Carrie moving about in the room above me, and later on the sound of a toilet being flushed; then everything was quiet. I have never been a particularly nervous person, but all at once I did not like the idea of being alone on the third floor, with the empty, locked bedroom next to me. I was about to get up out of bed and lock my own door—against whom or what I couldn't say—when I heard the characteristic click the door-knob made whenever the door was being opened. I froze for a moment, and then flung myself out of bed in a panic. By the time I found the matches and got the oil lamp lighted, my door was closed again, and no sound came from anyplace.

I stood perfectly still for a moment or two, staring at the doorknob, knowing that even if I turned the key now, and kept the lamp burning all night long, I would not be able to sleep. I sat down on the side of the bed, and took deep breaths until the thumping of my heart diminished and I felt that I had control of myself.

I tried to tell myself that a draft must have caused the door to try to open, or that I hadn't closed it tight before preparing for bed, but when I looked down I saw that my hands were clenched and my knuckles white. A few moments later I moved silently across the room, opened the door quickly, and after closing it behind me, sped barefoot along the hall and down to the floor below, where I knocked softly on the door of the study.

10

At the breakfast table the next morning I glanced several times at the faces around me for any hint of the identity of the person who had tried to enter my room in the middle of the night. I think William was doing the same thing, because he made a point of inquiring how each one had slept. They all seemed quite as usual, Agatha sending Bridget out for more cornbread and for strawberry preserves instead of the orange marmalade that was on the table, Aunt Carrie warming her hands on the coffeepot, Cousin Arthur reading the book review in the *Times,* and Millie, her sweet face still pale from her illness, quietly sipping the India tea she preferred to coffee. It all seemed so normal that I began to wonder if I hadn't, after all, had a bad case of nerves and imagined the click of the doorknob.

Later, when I went into the kitchen to see about the grocery order, I found Cook making a lengthy list of things that would be needed for what she called the funeral meats.

"People will be expectin' it, ma'am, when they come back to the house afterwards," she said. "Best be prepared."

"Oh, yes, of course," I said, although I had given no thought at all to the matter.

"Cold meat, aspics, salads, hot breads, and cakes," she said, nodding her head. "Oh, yes, and of course, relishes for the meat; I have plenty of them in the larder. And Mr. William will take care of the wine, no doubt."

She looked at me for affirmation before going on.

"Mrs. Cobb, ma'am, do ye have a minute? Sit down, do; you look more'n a bit weary." And she pulled the rocker up for me.

"I'm all right, Mrs. Murray. It's just the shock."

"Of course it is, ma'am, and you've been wonderful calm. I don't like asking you, but the girls have been at me—will you be wantin' us to stay on now that the master's gone?"

"Why, of course, Mrs. Murray. What on earth would I do without you? Tell Bridget and Nora not to worry . . ." I stopped, suddenly remembering that I was to go to Chicago with William.

"And the Misses Cobb, ma'am? Are they to live with us now? Because if that's the case . . ."

"Absolutely not, Mrs. Murray. They'll be leaving as soon as the funeral is over, if not before. I know it's not been easy for you, all the extra meals and trays . . ."

"Oh, it's not the food, ma'am. That never bothers me. It's her, Miss Agatha—into everything, demandin' to know why this and why that—"

"I know, I know," I said placatingly, thinking of the sal volatile. "And you've been so good about it all. I'll speak to Mr. William and see how soon we can send them off. Now, let me take your list upstairs, and I'll telephone the grocer and the butcher. Have you enough eggs for the omelettes for lunch?"

She gave me the list, but I was in no hurry to leave the comfort of the kitchen; the warmth, the savory smell of the beef broth simmering on the stove, the basket of green apples on the red-checked tablecloth, and the large gray and white cat sitting on the window seat staring out at the rain all combined to produce a mood of tranquility, so different from the nervous, unsettled atmosphere on the floors above. I would have liked to spend the morning there, but Cook's talk of funeral meats reminded me that I had better go through my wardrobe and see what I had that would be most suitable to wear to the ceremony. There would be no time to shop for something new.

Fortunately I had one black dress, one Henry had not cared for, and which I seldom wore, but it would do, I thought, if I removed the white bengaline collar and cuffs. I had taken the dress from the armoire and was holding it up to see if it needed pressing when Nora knocked on the bedroom door.

"Beg pardon, ma'am, but Miss Millicent said not to disturb her to change the bed—and today's the day I should do her room up. She said she had a headache, and wanted to lie down, and was not to be disturbed. Shall I just leave it, ma'am?"

"Yes, Nora, of course. You can change the bed tomorrow; one day won't matter. Miss Millicent hasn't been well, you know . . ."

After the girl left, taking the black silk dress with her "to give it a touch of the iron," I wondered if Millie was having a relapse. I certainly hoped not; I was as anxious as Cook to get her and Agatha out of the house as soon as possible. Perhaps, I thought, Dr. Gillespie could have a look at her when he comes . . .

The doctor did not arrive until almost three o'clock in the afternoon, and when he did, he was accompanied by two policemen. I was astonished to see them, and even more astonished to hear William say, "Hello, Bernie," and shake hands with the younger of the two, while the older, rather dour-faced officer looked from one to the other of us with expressionless eyes in a way that made me want to shiver. Then Dr. Gillespie cleared his throat and began to speak:

"It has been found that Mr. Henry Cobb died of a massive dose of tincture of opium, administered by a person or persons unknown; therefore, there will have to be an investigation by the authorities—"

At that point Agatha screamed, just once; when the older officer made a slight move in her direction she put her hand over her mouth and sat back. He kept his eyes on her for a moment, and then announced that no one was to leave the premises until further notice, and that each one of us would be interviewed and questioned.

"This does not necessarily mean that one of you is responsible for Mr. Cobb's death," he said, as if to soften the blow that stunned us all, "but since he died of opium poisoning, I am required by law to leave no stone unturned in an effort to determine whether the death was accidental or not. My name, by the way, is Lieutenant Broderick, and this is Sergeant Shaw. If you will kindly remain here, I will call you one at a time for questioning after we have gone through the rest of the house."

I couldn't believe what I was hearing; we, or one of us, were suspected of murdering Henry! I glanced across the parlor at William, who, judging from his look of intense concentration, was reviewing in his mind everything that had happened since he found his father's body. Agatha, for once, was speechless, and Millie, who was sitting quietly near the window, merely shook her head from time to time. Aunt Carrie fiddled with the strings of her little bag, and Cousin Arthur kept crossing and recrossing his legs. What a sorry-looking group of suspects we must have made.

Broderick went to the front door and beckoned to two more policemen, who came in carrying various pieces of equipment with them. Dr. Gillespie took them directly upstairs, and from time to time we could hear them moving about, opening and closing doors. After about half an hour the doctor left (without speaking to any one of us), and a few minutes later Broderick and Shaw came downstairs and asked William to provide them with a room for the interviews.

One by one we were called into the study; even the maids and Cook were questioned. I have no idea what the others were asked, or what their answers might have been, but I could add nothing to what I had already said to Dr. Gillespie the day before. Lieutenant Broderick did the questioning, while Sergeant Shaw sat at one side of the desk taking notes.

"You say you left your husband's room about half past nine, Mrs. Cobb. Did anyone see you leave?"

"Yes," I answered. "Millie, Miss Millicent Cobb, was on her way upstairs to the floor above. She said she was tired—she'd been ill—and would retire early."

"Then where did you go? To your own room?"

"No. It was still early. I went down to the parlor. Agatha—Miss Cobb—asked me to have some warm milk sent up to her, and after she left, William and I talked for a moment or two; actually, we just said good night. When I went up, Agatha was coming out of my room; she said she had been looking for some sal volatile in my bathroom."

Since the lieutenant made no comment before dismissing me, I had no way of knowing whether he believed me or not; his face, eyes, and voice had remained without expression during the entire interview.

It seemed to go on and on, the questioning, I mean, and when at last at the end of that long, long day the officers left, they took with them every bottle of medicine, every headache powder, every jar of pills in the house.

"How did you happen to know Sergeant Shaw?" I asked William as we sat over the fire late that night after the others had gone upstairs. "You greeted him like an old friend."

"He was at Columbia with me; he started out in engineering, and then decided he wanted to be a lawyer. I imagine he took a job on the police force to help him pay his way through law school. We were pretty good friends for a while, and then our paths diverged. I like him a hell of a lot better than Broderick."

"I didn't mention what happened last night, William, did you?"

"You mean about your coming downstairs to me?" he asked with a smile.

"You know I don't mean that! No, about the click of my doorknob; I was afraid he'd think me an idiot. I've been wondering if I imagined it . . ."

"No, I didn't mention it. But whether you imagined it or not is beside the point, my darling. You were frightened half to death, and tonight I want—"

"No, William, I will not give in to nerves. Tonight I'll lock the door, and I'm so tired, I'm sure I'll sleep."

It took me a while to convince him I was serious about overcoming my fear, and even so, he insisted on seeing that the lock on my door was in working condition.

"There's a definite click here," he said, turning the knob. "Are you sure you want to—"

"Yes, William dear, I am sure. Now, you must go. Kiss me good night . . ."

In spite of my brave words, I *was* nervous, and decided to leave the gas logs on in the fireplace so that I would not be in complete darkness. The glow they provided, though cheerful and comforting, was not bright enough to keep me awake, and what with the lateness of the hour and exhaustion from the strain of the day, I fell into a deep, heavy sleep almost at once.

I remember the dream; I'm sure that if I live for a century, I shall not forget it: in it I was swimming in the bay, with William next to me telling me how to kick properly, to use my legs as well as my feet, when suddenly I felt I couldn't breathe. I tried to cry out, to tell William my head was underwater, and then I awoke with a start, realizing that I *really* could not breathe, that something was being pressed down firmly on my face. My arms were useless—I could not get them out from under the bedclothes—but I could move my legs (the dream?), and with a tremendous effort I managed to turn my hips and roll over to the other side of the bed, where I lay gasping for air. I could see no one in the room.

As soon as I had command of myself, I got out of bed and checked the door; the key was in the keyhole, but it was not turned to the locked position, which meant that whoever tried to smother me had moved quickly, hastening out of the room and closing the door as soon as I began to struggle. And whoever it was must have been concealed someplace in the room, or in the bathroom, when I went to bed.

I was too frightened to go down to William for help, too terrified of the dimly lighted halls and stairs, and of what or who might be out there waiting for me. I relocked the door, lighted all three of my oil lamps, and after wrapping myself in a comforter, sat in the armchair next to the window and waited for the dawn. It was only half past two in the morning, and the minutes passed incredibly slowly. After a while I got up, and taking a block of writing paper from my drawer, I made a list that went approximately as follows:

WILLIAM: It couldn't have been he. He loves
                  me and wants to marry me.

AUNT CARRIE: Definitely not. She's afraid of the
                  dark and hates to leave her room at
                  night. But could she have gone
                  crazy? Her mind is not always clear.

COUSIN ARTHUR: I don't think so. He seems to be
                  fond of me, and he's a gentle man.
                  And what good would my death
                  do him?

MILLIE:	Out of the question: a frail, sweet woman, and besides, she's been sick.
AGATHA:	Possibly. Given to sudden rages, and could be considered unstable. She doesn't like me, either.
THE MAIDS:	No. Once up on their top floor for the night, nothing would bring them down.

An outsider? A prowler?

As I looked over the list I tried to imagine what reason each one would have for wanting me dead, and the only possible one I could come up with was that Agatha wanted so desperately to get control of Henry's money, or to be the mistress of this house, that she might—but wouldn't William inherit? And would he ever let her move in here?

My mind began to go around in circles; one moment I'd think it couldn't have been any one of them, not even Agatha, and in the next decide that I could rule out nobody, not even William. He could have thought that Henry had left me his entire fortune. At that point I knew I was too exhausted to think straight. I folded the sheet of paper and put it under a pile of handkerchiefs in my bureau drawer, and when I saw a faint light in the eastern sky I went back to bed. I slept immediately, and did not awaken until Nora knocked to tell me it was eleven o'clock, and that I was wanted in the study.

I dressed quickly in the plain black silk, thinking it would be appropriate if visitors called that afternoon offering condolences, and hurried downstairs.

11

Lieutenant Broderick was sitting behind Henry's desk with Sergeant Shaw beside him when I entered the room. Both men stood up when I approached them, but neither asked me to be seated. I thought they looked serious, but then that was how they'd appeared the day before when I'd been interviewed. I noticed, however, that no papers were spread out on the desk and the sergeant's notebook was not in evidence. I suppose that should have warned me; perhaps not, though, since I knew nothing about how policemen worked.

We said good morning to each other, and then, without preamble, Lieutenant Broderick stated his business:

"Mrs. Cobb, I must ask you to come with us. You are being charged with the murder of Henry Cobb."

"I—what—why—" I stammered, catching hold of the edge of the desk for support.

"A bottle of laudanum, or tincture of opium, as it is known, was poured into Mr. Cobb's drinking glass. Traces of the drug were found in the empty glass. The bottle, the incriminating evidence, was found in the drawer of the table next to your bed. You had refilled it with plain water. Now, if you will come—"

William tried in vain to stop them in the front hall, and the last thing I saw as I left the house between the two policemen was the stricken look on his face as Broderick waved the warrant for my arrest at him.

★　★　★

I can hardly bear, even now, to review the events of the next weeks. I was taken to the Women's House of Detention, put in a chamber, or rather a cell, whose dreadful furnishings I do not want to think about, and held there without bail until the trial was over. With the exception of my lawyer, a Mr. Rhinehart, I was allowed no visitors during that time, and I was permitted to speak to him only through an iron grille. He told me that William had retained him on the advice of Mr. Atherton, of Atherton, Bodine and Dolan, the firm that handled Henry's affairs.

In the beginning I was too sick and miserable to be of any help to him; the prison food gave me stomach cramps as well as diarrhea, and the prison smells nauseated me. Nor could I sleep; the screams and shouts of the other inmates never seemed to cease, and one terrible night I was sure I heard the sound of someone being beaten. I spent the days huddled on the hard pallet in one corner of the cell, wrapped in the single dirty blanket allowed me, and my nights in practically the same position.

I suppose I was in a state of shock. I know that the first few times Mr. Rhinehart came, I could do no more than stare at him; I could hear what he was saying, but the words were meaningless. He was patient, though, and when I was able to concentrate he convinced me that I must make an effort to provide him with the facts he needed in order to defend me.

He was a man of medium height, with light brown hair parted in the middle, a permanently wrinkled forehead, dark blue-gray eyes, and given to wearing rather baggy suits. At first glance he did not inspire confidence, but as time went on, I began to realize how competent he was. There was a certain authority, perhaps command, in his voice, and the intensity with which he listened to me, his eyes never leaving my face, belied the casualness of his appearance.

"It was most unfortunate, Mrs. Cobb," he said in a sort of introductory way one morning, "that when you were arraigned you came up before Judge Strickler. He's an unusually hard man; almost anyone else on the bench would have granted bail. Now listen carefully: it is essential that I hear everything, no matter how trivial or unimportant, everything that happened from the time Mr. Cobb fell down the stoop until the time the body was found."

He let me talk without interruption at first, but when I explained why Dr. Gillespie had given me the laudanum, he stopped me.

"You say he warned you not to take more than two drops in a glass of water. Were you told to keep the bottle under lock and key?"

"No," I replied. "Nothing like that was said. I kept it handy in the drawer of my night table, which was closed, but not locked."

"But it was out of sight? No one going into your room would have seen it without making a search?"

"That's right. But the door to my room was open during the day . . ."

"So any member of the household could have gone in there when you were on another floor?"

"I suppose so . . ."

"How many times did you take the laudanum?"

"Only twice, I think. Oh, yes, I did give a dose to Nora . . ."

"Yes," he said. "She confirms that." He was silent for a moment. "And when the remaining contents of the bottle were analyzed, they were found to be nothing but plain water—what is it?"

"Of course! How stupid of me! That explains why the drug had no effect the last time I took it, the night of Henry's death. I thought I might have built up an immunity to it, but I couldn't have, so quickly, could I? And after taking it only once before."

"No, of course not," he answered. "As I see it, this is what happened: some person waited until you were occupied in another part of the house, and made the substitution of water for the laudanum, returning the bottle to the exact position in which you had left it. Then he or she waited until you left Mr. Cobb sleeping, and poured the drug into the glass you had placed within his reach, first removing enough water—probably poured it back into the carafe—to accommodate the laudanum. When Mr. Cobb woke up feeling thirsty, he drank the whole glassful.

"As for the attempt on your life—how I wish you could point a finger there—that clears you entirely, in my mind, at least. Whether or not a jury would believe you is another matter; you have no proof, and it might sound fabricated. I won't bring it up unless I have to. I would rather base the defense on the lack of conclusive evidence. I want the jurors to be left with reasonable doubt."

We went over and over these points, so that I would be prepared for the questions asked by the prosecuting attorney and able to answer them without stumbling. The day before the trial started we had one last review, and when that was over, Mr. Rhinehart sat back and nodded confidently at me.

"You and I know I did not kill Henry, Mr. Rhinehart," I said, as he put his papers together. "But we don't know—"

"No," he said, "we do not know who did it. I have no evidence that points to any other member of the household. But my job now is to prove that *you* did not commit the murder, and I do not believe the jury will find you guilty. There is no real proof, only suspicion, and that is not enough to convict you."

* * *

He was right; three days later I was acquitted on the grounds of insufficient evidence. William and Cousin Arthur, who had been in the courtroom each day, hurried me through the crowd of curious onlookers into a waiting cab and took me home.

12

I couldn't wait to discard every stitch of clothing I had worn during the trial. In prison I had been compelled to surrender my own things, and wear instead what they gave me, shapeless garments of coarse, heavy cotton that chafed my skin and never seemed clean. My own clothes were returned to me the morning I went to court, but they must have been stored in a damp bin or closet, for a strong smell of mildew emanated from them. There was also a tear in the shoulder seam of my black dress, which made me wonder if someone larger than I had been wearing it.

I thought I must be carrying the prison smell on myself as well, and once home again, I spent the better part of the afternoon washing my hair and scrubbing myself in the hot, scented bath Nora drew for me. Even then I wasn't sure I was as fresh and dainty as I should be.

In the prison I had had no access to a mirror, and when I first looked into my glass at home, I could hardly believe that the pale, thin face that looked back at me was mine. The eyes seemed enormous, the cheeks sunken, the lips rough and chapped. No wonder, I thought, that so many people died in prison, if a little over a month did this to me.

What a relief it was to put on clean, fresh-smelling silk undergarments, and a dress that I was sure no one else had worn! When I emerged from the dressing room, Nora was arranging a tray on the table in front of the gas logs, and William was standing in the doorway, smiling at me.

"Cook says to eat it all, ma'am," Nora said. "It's too thin you are, she says. And she'll send up your dinner later on if you would rather not come down. And is there anything special you'd fancy, ma'am?"

"Tell Cook I will come down, Nora, and thank her, but say that whatever she has planned for dinner will be fine. Oh, and Nora, will you take the clothes I left on the chair in the dressing room and throw them away? Don't give them to anyone; just put them in the trash barrel."

"I see Cook is trying to fatten you up," William said, coming over to join me in front of the fire as Nora left the room with those wretched clothes.

"You'll have to help me eat some of this," I said, looking at the plates of sandwiches and little cakes on the tray. "My goodness, there's even custard—William, do I look so awful?"

"You look wonderful, my darling. You're too thin, that's all. Perhaps a tonic would help. I'll call Gillespie . . ."

"Oh, not Gillespie, please! If I need a doctor, I'll send for Dr. Atwater; he is the one we had in Gramercy Park."

I had a number of questions I wanted to ask William, but when we finished eating he insisted that I rest until dinner-time.

"Later, darling, I'll bring you up-to-date on things, but I want to tell you this right away: I've been transferred permanently to the New York office, so I don't have to rush off to Chicago. Also, I have moved into Pa's room in order that you won't be alone on this floor. Now, stretch out on the bed, and let me put the coverlet over you."

There were just four of us at dinner that night, Aunt Carrie, Cousin Arthur, William, and I, although it seemed like more, since Cook and the two maids were all in and out constantly, making sure that everything was to my taste. I was touched by their show of affection for me, and made an effort to do justice to the food. Food! It tasted like ambrosia . . .

"There are several things you should know, darling," William said when we were alone in the parlor after the meal. "Here, let me put this cushion behind you; now, put your feet up. There! You're looking better already."

"Apparently Agatha and Millie are back in Tenth Street," I said when he was seated.

"Yes, and I've told them you are not to have visitors for at least a week. Aggie's still upset about the will, but God knows why, when Pa left her plenty." He paused for a moment to add some coals to the grate.

"I think she expected to inherit this house," he continued, "but he left it to me, and I'm not sure I even want it. But the big surprise, darling, is that he bought the house in Oyster Bay, and that goes to you."

"Oh, William! He knew I loved it . . ."

"Yes, and I think he was planning it as a surprise for you in June."

I couldn't speak for a moment for fear of breaking down.

"There were other bequests, of course," William went on. "Cousin Arthur and Aunt Carrie both receive annuities—I shall have to take care of hers for her—and there are trust funds for Aggie and Millie. Thank God Atherton, Bodine and Dolan will administer those. The bulk of the estate is divided, share and share alike, between you and me. I don't have the exact figure yet, but we should each have close to a million. No distributions will be made for a while, maybe not for several months, but in the meantime there are funds for running expenses, and of course, I have my salary."

"I still own the Gramercy Park house, William. I think I might like to move back there . . ."

We talked for a little while longer, but made no definite plans, nor did we mention the fact that Henry's murder remained unsolved. That came later.

It was still early, only a little after nine, when I went

upstairs to prepare for bed, which I did without enthusiasm, even though I was on the verge of exhaustion. The memory of what happened the last time I slept in that bed would not go away, and I did not know how to go about erasing it. I was standing in my nightgown, near the night table, looking down at the pillows when William called good night from the dressing room. When I did not respond immediately he opened the door, and a moment later led me into the back bedroom, where he held me in his arms throughout the night.

13

I had known Dr. Atwater most of my life, and when he came to see me the next morning, I was momentarily transported back to the modest bedroom in the Gramercy Park house to which he had been summoned when I was sick with measles or one of the other diseases of childhood. I hadn't seen him since my father's death three years earlier, but his greeting was so warm and friendly that I felt as if I'd been talking to him yesterday.

"Nothing wrong with you that rest and good food won't set right, Sarah," he said after examining me. "You are suffering from exhaustion and malnutrition. I'll prescribe a tonic, and recommend a diet for you to follow. Also, I advise you to rest, with your feet up, either in bed or on that chaise over there, for several hours a day."

He put his stethoscope and other instruments back into his satchel, and then leaned over and patted my hand gently.

"Try to put recent events out of your mind, child. Get on with your life, and leave the past to itself. No good ever came of dwelling on it."

I suppose it was good advice, but like most advice, easier to give than to take.

★ ★ ★

During the days that followed the doctor's visit I was waited on hand and foot; everyone in the house pampered me, coaxed me to eat, begged me to "rest up." Cousin Arthur kept me supplied with light reading, Cook sent up eggnogs, broths, and little delicacies between meals, and even Aunt Carrie brought down biscuits (some of them quite stale) from her room. And William watched over me as if I were some sort of fragile hothouse flower that might suddenly wither on the stem.

He didn't want to discuss the mystery of his father's death; I imagine Dr. Atwater had told him to try to help me put it out of my mind, but one night I insisted on talking about it.

"I try not to think about it, William," I said, "but it's like trying not to pay attention to a sore tooth. *We* know I did not kill Henry, but—"

"Who did? That's the big question, I know, darling," he said. "And I've been talking to Bernie Shaw about it. I had lunch with him the other day. He's not at all satisfied with the way the case was handled—told me that all Broderick wanted was a quick conviction, something that would look good on his record. Anyway, we both think that one possible answer is that it was one of the nurses . . ."

"William! Why would—"

"There again, we don't know. But it is possible that one or the other of them was disgruntled at the peremptory way Pa fired them, and wanted revenge. It's a theory, darling, and we have no way of proving it right now, but it certainly is possible. They had ample opportunity to come into your room, just a quick trip through the bathroom while you were at dinner . . ."

"But it happened after they left. Why would they wait? And how could they have done it then?"

"Obviously so that they wouldn't be suspected. They'd been gone several days when he died, probably working on other cases, and would have perfect alibis. And the day nurse had been given a key so that she could come at six in the morning without waking everyone up. She could have had the key duplicated . . ."

"But why would she attack me? I don't think any of this makes sense, William."

"Maybe not, darling. Bernie says she may have thought you suspected something. Anyway, I think we ought to leave it at that, at least for now. If we, Bernie and I, come up with anything else, I'll tell you. I don't think he's going to let the matter rest. And speaking of rest, come on, love, time for bed."

My strength returned steadily, and by the end of a fortnight I not only felt, but also looked, almost like my old self. The doctor gave me permission to resume my normal activities on the condition that I rest the moment I felt any fatigue.

"Short walks at first, my dear," he said. "The fresh air will be good for you, but take someone with you in case you feel a little weakness."

I did take Nora with me a few times when I went out to do a little shopping or just to walk in the April sunlight, but by the time another week had gone by, I felt completely able to be on my own, and ready to make plans for the future.

William and I had decided that we would move out to Oyster Bay for the summer, and wait until the following February to be married, when the customary year of mourning would be over. He thought it was silly to wait so long, especially since I continued to sleep in the back bedroom with him, but he finally agreed that it would be better if we observed the rules of propriety, outwardly at least. I don't think anyone in the household suspected that I spent my nights with William, and in any case, I was too much in love to care if they did. I was careful, though, to return to my own room before Nora brought up my breakfast tray. I didn't worry about the others; Aunt Carrie lived almost completely in a world of her own, and Cousin Arthur gave no indication of being even remotely interested in where anyone slept. And Agatha and Millie had not come near me since I returned from prison.

As I said earlier, everyone in the household was solicitous of my well-being, and seemed genuinely glad to have me home again. I think now that their complete acceptance of my innocence, their belief that I was unjustly accused, accounts for my assumption that the outside world would be of the same opinion. I should have known better, and had I seen the newspapers during and immediately after the trial, I would have realized that acquittal on the grounds of insufficient evidence does not remove suspicion from the public's mind.

William, from the kindest of motives, had seen to it that no newspapers were brought up to me during my convalescence, and by the time I recovered, the press was no longer interested in Henry Cobb's widow. Attention was centered on the life of a prominent actress who had been found stabbed in her dressing room.

Realization of the true state of affairs came suddenly, and without warning: Margaret Oliphant, who had just returned from a trip to France, called and asked me to meet her for lunch at the Madison Club one day early in May. She had wonderful news, she said, and I was to be the first to hear it.

"My whole life is changing, Sarah," she exclaimed over the phone, "and I'm the happiest woman in the world."

She did indeed look happy when I spotted her waiting for me in the club lobby; her eyes were dancing, and there was a glow about her that reminded me of how she looked when she was in love with Richard Ealing. She welcomed me with a warm hug and kiss, and then took my arm. I was so engrossed in watching her that I almost did not notice the silence that came over the dining room as we made our way to a table overlooking the Statuary Court. I remember thinking it strange that none of the women with whom I'd been on friendly terms greeted me, and being surprised that Emma McAllister averted her glance when I nodded to her. But a moment later we were seated, and Margaret was telling me that she was going to New Mexico, to a place called Taos, to marry Ronald Pate, her artist friend.

"It's a popular artists' colony, Sarah, painters, sculptors, potters, all sorts of talented people. And Mabel Dodge may move out there; she's in Mexico now with John Reed. Oh, you'd love it, Sarah! Such a wonderful climate, and those marvelous desert vistas, and picturesque adobe houses!"

When I asked her what her parents thought of it all, she shook her head.

"Of course they don't like it, but what can they do? I'm of age, and I have Grandmama's trust fund. I can't and I won't let them control my life; this isn't the Dark Ages, you know." Who is in control of my life? I wondered. First it was my father, then Henry, and now—society?

Margaret studied my face for a moment, and then leaned across the table and put her hand over mine.

"I read all about what happened when I was in Paris, Sarah; oh, I wish I could have been with you! I could have helped somehow or other. Anyway, I can be of help now, get you away from New York until the talk all dies down. Come to Taos with me, Sarah! It's a whole new world."

I thanked her and said I'd think about it, and we left shortly afterwards. I made myself walk slowly as we passed through the now nearly empty dining room, but I wanted nothing more than to hurry home, to be among people who paid no attention to what Margaret called "the talk."

The moment I saw Nora's face when she opened the door for me, however, I knew something was wrong there, too.

"The Misses Cobb are upstairs, ma'am," she whispered, "and Herself is creatin' somethin' fierce—"

She stopped when she saw Millie hurrying down the stairs, and retreated to the kitchen.

"Oh, Sarah dear," Millie said breathlessly, grasping my hand in both of hers, "don't, please don't take any heed of what Aggie says. It's not what *I* think at all—oh, my dear, you'd best go into the study. Don't let her see you."

"What on earth—what is she doing upstairs?" I asked.

"If you must know," Agatha's voice came from above, "I came to look for a dressing sacque I thought I left in William's closet. It's not there. I suppose the maids—"

"Aggie! You know the maids wouldn't take it!" Millie pleaded.

"I know nothing of the sort. And why, pray, has William moved down to my brother's room? WHAT IS GOING ON IN THIS HOUSE?"

When I made no reply, she picked up her gloves and purse from the hall stand before turning to face me.

"I'd think your common sense would tell you, Sarah, that there's enough being said about you without adding immorality to the list. As it is, I could hardly hold my head up at my Tuesday night meeting, even though I made it clear that I, for one, have no intention of associating with a person whose reputation is as sullied as yours. You are a disgrace to the family."

With that, she flounced out of the house and left me to close the door behind her.

"Now sit down and tell me what it is that's bothering you, darling," William said, coming into my room after dinner that evening and closing the door. "I knew the moment I came home tonight that something was wrong."

I hesitated for a moment, not wanting to worry him unnecessarily, but in the end I told him everything that had happened, how I'd been shunned at the Madison Club, how

Margaret urged me to stay with her in New Mexico until the talk died down, and how Agatha vilified me.

"Of all the nasty, evil women—if I could get my hands on her—oh, darling, don't cry, don't. She doesn't know what she's talking about. Put it out of your mind."

"Can't you see what this means, William?"

"One thing it means is that she'll stay out of our lives from now on," he said, smiling grimly.

"That's not the important thing," I said slowly. "Surely you see that now it will be impossible for us to marry, don't you?"

"Why? Look here, Sarah: I love you, darling, and I don't care a fig—"

"Yes, I know you love me now, but how do I know that the day won't come when you, too, suspect me? Answer me, how do I know that?"

"You have my word, my solemn promise . . ."

"Now," I interrupted him. "That's *now*. What about ten, twenty, thirty years hence?"

"Sarah darling, believe me, I trust you as I trust myself. I will always trust you." He tried to take me in his arms, but I pulled away from him.

"William dear, listen to me. I spent most of the afternoon thinking about our situation. I cannot marry you; you would be snubbed, your career would be ruined, and in time you would blame me for that. I shall have to leave, that's all. Agatha knows you're using Henry's room—I told you what she said, and it won't be long before I'm known as a scarlet woman as well as a suspected murderess."

"I won't have it, Sarah! There must be another way— where would you go?"

I had given some thought to this question during the hours I spent alone that afternoon, and decided I had three choices: I could accept Margaret's offer, I could return to the Gramercy Park house as soon as the present lease expired, or I could move out to Long Island. I told William I had settled on the Oyster Bay house, since it was secluded, almost isolated, thus making it unlikely that I would run into people who knew me. He protested that I'd be all alone, that I wouldn't be safe, and so on, but in the end I convinced him that it was the wise thing to do.

"Sarah, look at me," he said, putting his hands on my shoulders and turning me to face him. "Tomorrow I'll see Bernie Shaw again; as I told you before, he's *very* interested in the case, and I intend to impress him with the importance of finding the person who attacked you, because if we can do that, we'll have the murderer."

"Bernie Shaw might not believe you about the attack on me, William. Mr. Rhinehart was afraid to make any mention of it at the trial for fear the jury would think I had made the whole thing up. Sometimes I think I might have dreamed it myself—had a nightmare. I was terribly upset about Henry at the time . . ."

"But Rhinehart believed you, didn't he? And Bernie will, I have no doubt. Somehow or other I am going to clear your name, once and for all, and then we'll get married if I have to abduct you."

I smiled at him, and said I had something to show him. I went over to my bureau and took out the folded sheet of paper from underneath my handkerchiefs, and handed it to him. He frowned as he read it, then looked up and grinned at me.

"I'm happy to see that you exonerated me, darling," he said. "I'll show this to Bernie. Maybe it will give him some ideas. By the way, did you know that his name really is Bernard Shaw? But he wasn't named for the playwright; he told me his mother read a life of a Saint Bernard—of Clairvaux, I think—before his birth, and thought he was one of the greatest . . ."

★ ★ ★

I had intended to sleep in my own room that night, so that William would know that I wouldn't be afraid to be on my own in Oyster Bay, but after I had undressed, he came in, picked me up, and carried me into his bed.

14

May 15, 1913

My dearest Sarah,

I was glad to hear that you are so comfortably established in Oyster Bay. Are you sure you can manage with only Nora to help you? The thought of the two of you alone in that big house makes me uneasy. Be careful, darling, about locking up at night, will you?

I am making some progress here; Bernie is being extremely cooperative, since he wants to get to the root of the matter almost as much as I do. Broderick is out of it completely: Bernie thinks he got quite a dressing down for making a false arrest. We have gone over all the facts again and again, and have decided on one thing at least: to eliminate the possibility that it was a prowler or anyone outside the household. Bernie is not keen on the theory that it might have been one of the nurses, but he hasn't discarded it yet.

By the way, I showed him your list of suspects, but so far he has made no comment on it. We have come up with a plan of sorts, and when we've worked out the details I'll write and explain it to you.

You can't possibly know how much I miss you, my darling.

> All my love,
> William

I folded the letter back into its envelope, and sat for a while on the verandah, letting the warmth of the May sun and the scent of the freshly cut grass wash over me, more relaxed than I'd been since Henry's death. The move out to the north shore of Long Island had been a surprisingly easy one; since Henry had bought the house completely furnished, I had only my personal possessions to transport. I thought that in the future I would have some redecorating done, but for the time being I was content to leave things as they were.

I was rested, too; there was no one to make demands on my time, so I could garden, or swim, or walk along the water's edge whenever I felt so inclined. There was also time for me to write, and no one to interrupt me as I worked on my little stories for children. Even Nora hesitated to call me for lunch when she saw me sitting at the old-fashioned rolltop desk in a room off the kitchen that must once have served as an office of some sort.

As William said in his letter, it was a large house, far too spacious for just the two of us, but after I closed off four of the bedrooms and two bathrooms, Nora managed to keep up with the rest. I had persuaded her, but not without some difficulty, to sleep in the room adjoining mine, instead of in the servants' wing as she had the previous summer. At first she demurred—it wouldn't be right, she said—but when I told her that Mr. William wanted me to have someone within call in case I felt ill during the night, she agreed, and insisted on putting the dinner bell next to my bed.

"That way I'll be sure to hear you, ma'am, and anyway, we won't be needin' it 'less we have company."

It also took some coaxing to get her to sit down at the table with me in the breakfast room, where we had our meals instead of in the formal dining room.

"Mrs. Murray said she'd have my head, ma'am, if I let you lose weight again, and the Lord knows what she'd do if she saw me eatin' with you."

"She need never know, Nora," I said, watching her blue Irish eyes light up. She wasn't much of a conversationalist, but she was a pleasant person to have around; nothing was too much trouble for her, partly, I think, because she was by nature energetic, and partly because she was genuinely enjoying life in the country.

Since the property that came with the house was extensive, ten or twelve acres, I believe, there were no near neighbors, and with the exception of the gardener and his nephew, who came every Friday to tend the grounds, and the boys who delivered the groceries, we saw no one. I had been concerned at first that Nora might miss her city friends, but if she did, I saw no sign of it other than noticing that on Fridays she made a point of weeding the vegetable garden when Joseph, the gardener's nephew, was working in that area.

William wrote to me three or four times a week, love letters for the most part, with only occasional and not very specific references to the plan he and Sergeant Shaw were evolving. Then toward the end of June he telephoned, saying it was imperative that he see me.

"I know we agreed not to meet until the murder is solved, Sarah, but I must see you face-to-face and discuss this plan of ours with you. I can be there tomorrow evening, darling, and I'll have to leave the next afternoon. Don't count on me for dinner either day," he said. The excitement in his voice was contagious, and after he hung up I felt incapable of anything but impatient anticipation.

It was dark when I heard the village taxi come up on the gravelled drive in front of the house, but even so, I didn't dare go out on the verandah to greet him. I was afraid I might hurl myself at him in full view of the driver. This turned out to be a wise precaution on my part, because I would not have cared to have a witness to our passionate embrace. When William released me, we stood for a moment, wordless, looking at each other, then still without speaking, we turned and went upstairs.

In the morning after Nora had served us a hearty breakfast of fresh fruit, cornbread, and bacon and eggs, and after William had teased her about the report he would make to Mrs. Murray about her cooking, we took our second cups of coffee out to the garden. I held William's for him while he dragged two lawn chairs out of the gardener's shed, and when we were seated next to a bed planted with petunias and verbena, he explained what he and Bernie Shaw planned to do.

"This may sound overly dramatic—melodramatic, maybe—but hear me out, darling, and then tell me what you think. I proposed to Bernie, and he finally agreed that it's worth a try, a reenactment of what took place the night Pa died. That means that you and Nora will have to come to the city for a day or two."

"Of course, William, but what about Agatha? She should be there, and she won't come if I'm there."

"That's where we'll have to resort to trickery; you know how anxious she's always been to spend time in the Forty-ninth Street house, don't you? Well, I'll arrange for her to do just that, but in order to make sure that she and Millie move in there at a particular time, we'll have to employ a bit of subterfuge. We will have their house on Tenth Street declared unsafe, at least for a short period of time."

"How on earth will you do that?"

"Easily. Bernie will arrange for a building inspection (bogus, of course) of Aggie's house and a couple of neighboring ones as well, to make it look legitimate. A gas leak will be found in the basement, and Aggie will be asked to go down and sniff it—they'll spill some stuff around that smells like illuminating gas.

"I shall make a point of being there: Millie's been after me any number of times to drop in for tea, so I'll have an excuse. The inspector, a friend of Bernie's, will insist that the house be vacated at once for fear of an explosion, and I'll take the aunts home with me."

"You are being devious, William."

"Devious, but not criminal; I do not intend to kill anyone, but I must find out who poisoned Pa and tried to smother you. Let me finish: you will come into town unexpectedly, a sudden toothache or something like that, and I will be surprised to see you established in your own room when I return with Agatha and Millie.

"That night each one will sleep in the room he or she occupied the night of the murder, with one exception: I will pretend to go to bed in the study, where I slept then, but in reality I'll sleep in my father's room."

"Thank heavens," I murmured.

"So," he went on, "Cousin Arthur and Aunt Carrie will be in their own rooms, you in yours, Millie in the spare room next to Aunt Carrie, and Aggie in my old room on the fourth floor."

"But, William, Agatha *knows* you've been sleeping in Henry's bed. She said—"

"Yes, I know, but I'll just say the study is cooler in the summer. Now listen: during dinner Bernie will come in. He will have a key to the front door, and he'll take charge of things from then on. He's still working out the details."

I could not see how anything could be accomplished by such a charade, and judging from William's next remark, I must have looked more than a little bit skeptical.

"I know it seems like grasping at straws, Sarah darling, and I had trouble convincing Bernie that it was worth a try. If he wasn't an old friend of mine, and if it didn't bother him that the murder was unsolved, I don't think he would have agreed to go along with me. He finally consented when I reminded him of the scene in *Hamlet*, the reenactment of the death of Hamlet's father by the players. 'The play's the thing wherein I'll catch the conscience of the king.' Remember?"

I nodded, and he kissed me lightly before continuing.

"The idea is, just as in Shakespeare's play, to watch everyone closely, 'observe his looks,' as Hamlet says of the king during the performance. Only, in this case we'll observe the looks of several people. And who knows? Someone may

> *"'Have by the very cunning of the scene*
> *Been struck so to the soul that presently*
> *They have proclaimed their malefactions.'"*

He recited the lines in such a dramatic stage whisper that I had to smile. "I didn't know you were so well versed in Shakespeare," I said.

"Memorized yards of it early in life," he responded, "and it's stayed with me. Look, darling, I know it's a long shot, but I can't think of anything else, and it's better than doing nothing. Someone is guilty of murder, and I will try anything to find out who it is. Then justice will be done, and your name will be clear."

He was so excited about doing something, taking action of any sort, that I agreed to do my part, although I did not feel at all enthusiastic about a trip to the city and a night in that house. I almost asked him to give it all up and stay with me when he kissed me good-bye that afternoon, but of course I didn't.

15

When Nora and I were alone again I had plenty of time to go over in my mind what William had proposed, and the more I thought about his plan, the more doubtful I became of its chances of success. I knew as well as he did that the only way of clearing me of any lingering suspicion in the public's mind was to find and expose Henry's murderer, but I could not see how gathering us all under one roof for a single night and simulating the conditions that prevailed that night in February would be of much help. As William said, it was grasping at straws . . .

Of course, I had no way of knowing just what Sergeant Shaw had in mind, but I *did* know that he had not demurred when Broderick arrested me, and I could not help wondering whether, in spite of everything, he still thought me guilty. My acquittal might not have convinced him of my innocence, and if he was still of the opinion that I had put the laudanum in Henry's water glass, he could be concentrating on trying to entrap me.

I shuddered at the thought of those sharp eyes of his following my every move, waiting for me to do or say something that would give me away. William had assured me that I could not be tried twice for the same crime, but I knew that cases could be reopened if some new evidence came to light—and Bernie Shaw was looking for that evidence.

I began to dread the prospect of a night in the Forty-ninth

Street house, and even went so far as to start a letter to William saying I simply could not go through with it, and that they would have to manage without me. I never finished writing it, though, and when he phoned to say that everything was set for Tuesday, July 7, I agreed to be there by three o'clock in the afternoon at the latest. I even made an appointment with our old dentist on East Nineteenth Street for that morning. I had no toothache, but I knew that Dr. Burns would be happy to see me and check the condition of my teeth. That way, I reasoned, if any questions were asked about my presence in the city, Nora would be able to corroborate my story.

I had thought she'd welcome a trip into town, and was therefore somewhat surprised at her lack of enthusiasm when I mentioned it to her. At first she looked a bit downcast, but when I said we'd probably be coming back the next day, she brightened up considerably, and it occurred to me that she would not have liked being away on a Friday, when Joseph and his uncle came to do the heavy gardening. Later on, when I told William that we might be in danger of losing Nora to the gardener's nephew, he laughed, and said that if that happened, we'd hire Joseph too, and have a fine couple to do for us.

Tuesday dawned hot and still; I doubt that we could have picked a worse day to travel to the city. The heat in the train was almost unbearable, and opening the windows next to our seats did no good at all, since soot and cinders from the engine up ahead blew in, adding to our discomfort. Fortunately it was not a very long ride from Oyster Bay to the Pennsylvania Station.

"I can send you directly up to the house, Nora, if you'd like," I said as we were making our way over to the taxi ramp on the Thirty-third Street side. "There's no need for you to come down to the dentist's with me." But she would have none of that.

"Oh, no, ma'am. I'd better stay with you. Supposin' you

was to feel faint in this heat? What would Mr. William say to me if I'd left you alone?"

So we rode together in a rattly taxi cab down to Nineteenth Street, past sights familiar to me since childhood, and when we reached the dentist's office I asked the driver to wait, hoping that Dr. Burns would not keep me too long.

It has been said over and over again that New Yorkers thrive on change, that old buildings must be replaced with new ones, or at least altered in some fashion, that the most desirable neighborhood is the newest one, that what was the dernier cri one year is passé the next, in short, that whatever is new is best. Dr. Burns, obviously, was not of that mind; the office into which he ushered me had not, as far as I could see, changed in the slightest detail in all the years I had been his patient.

The same faded turkey carpet covered most of the hardwood floor, the same lace curtains and reddish brown velour drapes hung at the windows, and the same large mahogany chest, with its dozens of little drawers, each with a cut-glass knob, stood against an inner wall. The elaborately upholstered wrought-iron patient's chair occupied the center of the room, and over it hung the traditional dentist's light fixture on a pulley, so that it could be raised and lowered. To the left of the chair, on an outside wall, lion-headed andirons stood in a cozy brick fireplace, surmounted by a mantel on which rested a marble bust of Aesculapius. In a corner near the window, a cluttered rolltop desk held an array of account books and texts. I remember how comforting the warmth from the smouldering logs in the fireplace used to feel on my feet on a snowy afternoon as I sat with my head back and my mouth open for inspection. It wasn't at all like being in a doctor's office; it was more like being in a room in someone's house that just happened to have a dentist's chair in it.

"Your teeth are fine, my dear Sarah," Dr. Burns said, as he put his instruments away. "You're a bit thin, which isn't surprising after what you went through last winter, but you look well." He paused for a moment, as if gathering his thoughts. "Don't pay any attention to what people say, child. Hold your head up. New York will forget all about you as soon as the next sensation comes along, if it hasn't already forgotten."

I wanted to believe him, but as I said good-bye, I couldn't help thinking of the long memories some people have. In any case, I did not want to be forgotten; I wanted to be exonerated.

The driver had waited, and was happy to take us slowly around the perimeter of Gramercy Park, while I pointed out some of the landmarks to Nora. The house in which I had grown up, and which I still owned, looked deserted, with the shutters closed and the blinds drawn, but since I'd had no word from the rental agent that the tenants had departed, I assumed that they were away for the summer. The little park itself was almost empty; aside from an elderly man sitting on a bench, fanning himself with a newspaper, and a tired-looking maid walking a dog just outside the railing, I saw nobody. Dark green leaves hung limply in the still air, and the hot sun glinted off the Water Nymph Fountain, nullifying any effect of coolness the little cascade of water provided. Gramercy Park was definitely not at its best that day.

In times past, had we been in town on such a day, my father would have waited until the sun was low in the sky behind Calvary Church before calling me to accompany him on a leisurely stroll through the park and its environs. I can see him yet, a slim, elegant figure, meticulously and formally dressed, no matter what the weather, walking slowly, pausing now and again to point with his malacca cane at an architectural detail on one of the buildings. He commented often, and at length, on the beauty and variety of the doorways of the older houses, and several times lamented the loss of the elaborate entrance designed by Calvert Vaux for Number 15, the Tilden house. It had been removed when the mansion was converted into the National Arts Club in 1905.

"At least they didn't touch the bay windows," he would say, shaking his head, "but why they destroyed that magnificent doorway, I'll never understand. It was a work of art, and should have been preserved. Whoever ordered it demolished ought to be executed; prison would be too good for such a scoundrel."

Remembering his words, I had to wonder what effect my imprisonment would have had on him, had he lived. Would he, I asked myself as we rode uptown, have reacted like Agatha? Would he have felt that I had disgraced the Cunningham name, too? Maybe it's just as well that I'll never know.

Our reception at the city house was almost royal; Cook, Bridget, Cousin Arthur, and Aunt Carrie were genuinely delighted to see us, and full of concern about my toothache, even after I assured them that Dr. Burns had taken care of it.

Aunt Carrie recommended oil of cloves, Cousin Arthur cold compresses, Cook said a tablespoonful of whiskey held in the mouth never failed to help, and Bridget told how her old Mam in Ireland used to tie a piece of flannel around her head. Only with difficulty did I convince them that I was without pain, but even so, Cook, when she realized we'd had no lunch, insisted on plying me with soft foods: cold leek soup, an omelette, and chocolate pudding. "So you needn't be chewin' on the sore tooth, Mrs. Cobb."

They were all so affectionate and considerate that for a little while I was able to put aside thoughts of the real reason for my visit. Later on, though, when I was alone in my room, I had trouble keeping my mind off the night ahead. I tried telling myself that by this time tomorrow I'd be safely back in the garden in Oyster Bay, perhaps with William beside me, but even that prospect failed to dispel the anxiety I could feel building up within me.

It was only half past two, and to pass the time I dallied in a cool bath and took my time dressing. The flowered voile dress I had brought with me, one left over from the previous summer, hung nicely from the shoulders, and was ever so much more comfortable than the travel suit I had worn into the city. If it hadn't been for the worried look in my eyes, I think I would have been pleased with the reflection I saw in the pier glass that hung between the windows. My skin was clear, my color good, and my long brown hair, which I piled up on top of my head to keep it off my neck, had a few golden glints in it from the sun—not unbecoming at all.

The afternoon seemed to stretch endlessly ahead of me; I tried to doze on the chaise longue, but my mind was far too active to allow for a beneficial rest. Nor could I concentrate on a novel I had started to read before moving out to Long Island. I was almost at my wits' end when I suddenly remembered that I had left a half-written story in the little desk Henry had given me, and hurried down to find it. The curtains in the study had been closed partway against the afternoon sun, and in the dim light I did not immediately see Cousin Arthur standing in front of the bookshelves to the right of the fireplace. I must have gasped, because he turned around quickly to face me with an apologetic look.

"Oh, Sarah, I'm sorry if I startled you. Is your tooth better? I was just looking to see if Henry had a copy of Whitman's Civil War poems. I seem to have mislaid mine, and there's a reference I need to check."

"I'll help you look," I said, and pulled back the curtains. I found the volume on the other side of the room, near the door, and he went off with it under his arm. I was about to look for my unfinished story when I noticed that the colors in the little painting that so resembled a Monet garden scene were glowing in the light I had let into the room. I went over for a closer look, and as I straightened the picture—it was slightly askew—I realized why it was so familiar to me. The narrow path, the roses against the wall, and the little garden seat were just as I had seen them hundreds of times from the rear windows of the Gramercy Park house.

What Henry was doing with one of my father's paintings, I could not imagine. He'd never spoken of it, but that in itself was not strange, because as William had said, he'd never shown any interest in paintings or other works of art. The only thing I could think of was that he had bought it as an act of charity when my father's funds were low. I made a mental note to ask William if there was any reference to it in Henry's accounts, and gathered up my papers just as the front doorbell sounded. A moment later I heard Agatha's distinctive voice.

"What is Nora doing here, William? I thought you said she had gone to Oyster Bay with Sarah."

16

I was afraid Agatha would make a fuss about sitting at the same table with me and that she would insist upon having her dinner sent upstairs to her, but she contented herself with ignoring my presence, never once looking in my direction or addressing me. Millie, visibly embarrassed by her sister's behavior, tried to make amends.

"There's nothing so annoying as an aching tooth, Sarah dear. I've had my share of them. Did you try rubbing a little paregoric on the gum? That's what our old nannie used to do years ago. I remember—"

"It was not Nannie, Millie," Agatha broke in sharply. "It was that French one, the one who taught us deportment and how to conduct ourselves properly."

"And failed gloriously," Cousin Arthur muttered under his breath. Then he cleared his throat and asked Millie about the gas leak.

"Oh, we had such a very, very narrow escape, Arthur," she replied. "It was so fortunate that they were making an inspection today, and even more fortunate that William happened to be there."

"They said someone had reported an odor of gas out in the street, so they were checking all the houses in our row," Agatha said, helping herself to Parker House rolls. "And I shall demand a written guarantee that the proper repairs have been made before I set foot in that house again. Perhaps we should think of moving; do you realize that we might have been blown to bits, William?"

"Indeed I do, Aunt Aggie," he replied seriously. "But you can rest assured that it will be taken care of. I spoke to the chief inspector myself."

"It might be wise for us to stay here until we go to Lake Mohonk in August," Agatha said meditatively. "Yes, I think I'd feel safer here."

I did not dare look at Bridget, who was standing next to me, waiting to hand around the plates of English trifle I was serving. She and Cook will want to come back to Oyster Bay with me, I thought, if Agatha is to stay here for three weeks.

"Oh, they said they'd have it fixed by tomorrow, Aunt," William said quickly. "They can't afford to waste time. Why, they probably have it sealed off already."

"Well, I don't think I'll ever feel comfortable there again," Agatha said, picking up her dessert spoon. "Umm, this is very good, a nice change from green apple pie."

I don't remember the rest of the dinner table conversation, but I know that no mention was made of Sergeant Shaw, nor could I detect any sign of his presence in the house. I had had no opportunity to speak to William since he arrived with the sisters, with the result that I was almost as much in the dark as the rest of the household concerning the plans for the night.

Aunt Carrie, as was her custom, disappeared as soon as the meal was over, and Millie, saying she had slept poorly the previous night because of the heat, retired to the spare room shortly thereafter. William went up to the study to make some phone calls, and Cousin Arthur announced that since it seemed to be cooling off a bit, he would take a short walk.

"Need a little exercise to help me sleep," he said. "Would anyone care to join me?"

To my surprise, Agatha said a breath of fresh air was just what she needed, and quickly pinned on her hat.

"I enjoy a walk after dinner, Arthur," she said as he held

140

the door for her, "but I dislike being alone on the streets in the evening, and Millie is so lazy. Thank you, but you needn't take my arm."

As soon as the door closed on them, William beckoned to me to come into the study. He held me close to him for a moment or two, and then told me that Bernie Shaw was already in the house.

"He slipped in while we were at dinner. He's up in Pa's room, darling, and will be there all night. I'll be down here in the daybed—I know you wanted me upstairs near you, but you'll be all right with Bernie in the next room. His theory is that having all of us in the same positions we were in the night of the crime may bring it all back to the murderer, cause him to worry that he forgot something, left a clue. Then, thinking Pa's room is empty, he'll go back to rectify it."

"But it's been empty before," I protested.

"Not when Millie and Aggie were here. And no one knew about the night I spent with you in Oyster Bay. I said I'd be out for dinner that night, and late coming home. I even left a note saying I'd had to leave for the office extra early the next morning, so Arthur and Aunt Carrie wouldn't guess I hadn't been home all night. No, darling, no one ever knew, and this *is* the first night anyone might assume the room to be empty."

"William, suppose nothing happens at all?"

"Sarah dear, I know it's a wild scheme, but there is just a chance that it will work. After all, we know it has to be one of four people: Aggie, Millie, Arthur, or Aunt Carrie."

"But have you thought of *why* one of them would do it? I've been over it and over it in my mind and I can't. If it has to be one of them—and it must be—I'd suspect Agatha; remember I told you she was in my room pretending to look for the sal volatile? She may have been after the laudanum then."

"I agree with you that she's the most likely suspect, but we have no proof. We'll just have to wait and see if anything happens tonight."

"But, William, you forget that the room has been empty in the daytime, and Arthur and Aunt Carrie have been here."

"Yes, I know, but neither one of them is first on our list of suspects."

"And Agatha and Millie were here the day I had lunch with Margaret, remember? Agatha said she's been looking for her dressing sacque."

"Yes," he said slowly, "but not in Pa's room. Bridget was in there dusting or cleaning or something and said Aggie looked in the doorway and gasped and asked her what my things were doing in there. Please bear with me, darling. Just give this a chance."

We went on talking until Cousin Arthur and Agatha came in. I heard her call good night to him and say she was going down to the kitchen to see if there was any lobster salad left. A little while later William saw me up to my room, kissed me good night, and went quietly down to the daybed in the study, leaving me to try to sleep in the bed I had come to loathe.

I was feeling frightened and irritable at the same time; frightened of what might happen in the dark, and irritated at having to go through a performance I thought was pointless. I was sure I would have trouble sleeping, but I guess the long, hot day had left me more physically tired than I realized, because I did not lie awake. I slept soundly, dreamlessly, until a series of raucous shrieks, not unlike the cries of the sea gulls on the Sound, jolted me into consciousness.

When I saw Agatha clinging to the newel post at the top of the stairs, alternately gasping for breath and screaming, my first thought was to find Millie. I remembered that Henry had said she was the only one able to calm her sister when

Agatha was seized with an uncontrollable rage. I brushed past Sergeant Shaw, who was standing, fully dressed, in the doorway to Henry's room staring at the distraught woman, and ran upstairs to the fourth floor clad only in my nightgown.

By the time I had roused Millie (how she could have slept through the noise I will never know) and hurried her down the stairs Agatha had slumped to the floor, and William and Cousin Arthur were bending over her. Shaw had retreated to the darkness of Henry's room, where he could not be seen from where we were gathered. The screams had been succeeded by a piteous moaning or wailing, which gradually ceased as Millie cradled her sister's head in her arms and crooned softly to her. Cook appeared from nowhere with a cup of brandy, but Agatha turned away from it and closed her eyes.

As we waited for Agatha to recover Aunt Carrie came halfway down the stairs and leaned over the banisters, wanting to know if there were burglars in the house. No one answered her. We all stared at Agatha as Millie continued to croon soothingly. Sergeant Shaw, unnoticed, watched from the doorway of Henry's room.

Agatha opened her eyes, and then tried to speak. I thought she said "my brother," but I couldn't be sure. A moment later her head dropped down on Millie's arm and she lay still.

Cook went down on her knees and began to pray.

17

We did not hear a full account of what took place in Henry's bedroom that night until after Agatha's funeral. She was buried in the Cobb family vault in the Woodlawn Cemetery on a hot, humid morning, with only the family and Sergeant Shaw in attendance. After the ceremony I invited him to come back to the house with us for the cold lunch Cook said she'd have ready. He had already told me that he was satisfied that Agatha was guilty of Henry's murder, and he had also apologized for having been part of the team that caused me to suffer imprisonment and the trial that followed.

Since I wanted no more notoriety than I'd already had, I was greatly relieved that instead of the headlines that I'd been told appeared in the paper when I was accused of Henry's murder, there was only a small box on one of the back pages of the *Times* informing the world of my innocence. A political scandal that was raging at the time was far more sensational than the clearing of my name. How right Dr. Burns had been when he said that New York quickly forgot.

Since William and I were the only ones who knew that Bernie Shaw had been in the house and had witnessed Agatha's death, Cousin Arthur, Millie, and Aunt Carrie were taken by surprise when he began to speak. He waited until the iced

144

coffee had been served and Bridget had withdrawn before he started.

He was lying in Henry's bed, he said, with the cover drawn up to conceal his street clothes, waiting to see if the guilty person would, for one reason or another, return to the scene of the crime. When nothing had happened by two o'clock in the morning, he was almost ready to admit his ruse had failed and to slip out of the house. He waited, though, still hoping, and at two twenty-five he heard footsteps in the hall. When the door slowly opened, letting in a faint light from the gas fixture in the hall, he lay perfectly still, holding his breath.

"She didn't see me at first," he said, glancing around the table at the intent faces of the listeners. "She went straight past the bed, over to the chiffonier in the corner near the windows. She opened one drawer after another, obviously looking for something, or rather, feeling for something; I could tell by the scrabbling sound her fingers made on the wood that there wasn't enough light for her to see clearly.

"I don't know what made her turn around, nervousness, or some little noise, probably, but when I heard her gasp I knew she had realized that someone was in the bed. I sat up slowly, keeping my face in the shadow so that she'd think I was her brother, or his ghost."

"Wouldn't she have thought it was William?" I asked. "He'd been using that room."

"No," William answered, "because I made a point of being sure she heard me ask Nora to make up the daybed in the study. I said I thought it would be cooler down there."

"In any case," the sergeant continued, "she *did* take me for Mr. Henry Cobb, or his ghost. She stayed where she was. She didn't scream just then; she made a funny sort of croaking sound and leaned forward to peer at me. I knew that her first words would be crucial, so I didn't move. I waited. In a moment or two she spoke—here, I've written down exactly what she said."

145

He took a small notebook from his pocket and read:

"Henry! Henry! But you are dead! The laudanum—too much—I didn't want you to die, Henry. I only . . ."

He closed the notebook and sat in silence for a moment.

"That was all. Then she began to scream like a banshee, and ran out into the hall. You know the rest. As Gillespie said, she died of an apoplectic stroke, and maybe it's just as well. Now she cannot be tried for the murder of her brother."

Millie sighed and sat back in her chair. She and Cousin Arthur had both been leaning forward during Shaw's recital, hanging on his words, and even Aunt Carrie seemed to be listening carefully, for once not fussing with her drawstring bag. There was a silence around the table for a few moments, and then Millie startled me.

"Was there really a gas leak, William?" she asked.

Before William could reply, Sergeant Shaw explained that it was his idea to set up a similar situation to the one that existed the night of Henry's murder.

"I couldn't think of any other way of getting you and your sister here without arousing your suspicion," he said. "And I must say I had my doubts that I could prove anything. But, as you have seen, the plan worked. It never occurred to me, though, that it would bring on apoplexy."

"All that lobster salad . . ." Cousin Arthur murmured.

"Aggie always ate too much," Millie said. "She'd been warned. But, Sergeant, what I cannot understand is *why* she went into Henry's room in the middle of the night."

"I think it was because she never had any other chance to go in there unobserved," I said. "She was certainly looking for something. Remember the day I came home unexpectedly early from lunch, when she was upstairs pretending to be looking for a dressing sacque she said she left here?"

"Obviously she was looking for something," Sergeant Shaw said somewhat impatiently. "And I postulate that she thought there was something in that chiffonier that might

146

incriminate her, and wanted to remove it. I, however, could find nothing of the sort there."

"Well, there wouldn't be," William said. "Those drawers are full of my things, except for a few odds and ends of Pa's, his watch, cuff links, things like that, which I left in one of the small drawers at the top. Oh, yes, there's an heirloom, a medal given my grandfather, your father, Aunt Millie, by President Lincoln at the end of the Civil War."

"I thought that was kept in the safe, William," Cousin Arthur said. "Henry promised to show it to me sometime, but never got around to it. Very valuable, he said."

"No," William said, shaking his head. "The letter of commendation, signed by Lincoln, is in the safe. Pa thought that was more precious than the medal. They should both probably be in the Smithsonian, or some other museum."

While William was speaking I suddenly had a picture of Cousin Arthur standing near the safe the day I went into the study to look for my unfinished manuscript, but my thoughts were interrupted by the sergeant's asking if we had any questions left.

"Yes," William said. "There's one for which I can find no answer: what possessed Aggie to make an attempt on Sarah's life, to try to smother her?"

I could tell by their expressions that Millie and Cousin Arthur and Aunt Carrie had not been told that someone had tried to kill me, but I said nothing, and the sergeant addressed himself to them.

"Miss Agatha Cobb was in Mrs. Cobb's room looking for the laudanum when Mrs. Cobb surprised her. She said she was hunting for some sal volatile, and put it off that way. But she'd had a fright—she knew her story was thin, and that Mrs. Cobb would probably suspect her. So she decided to silence her. She would have removed the pillow, and replaced it after you stopped breathing," he said, turning to me, "and no one would ever have known that you didn't die peacefully in your sleep. Remember, she had already committed one murder, and would have had no compunction about killing again. But what she didn't know was how long it takes to smother a person with a pillow. Fortunately, Mrs. Cobb, you managed to fight your way out before you were asphyxiated."

"Oh, dear God . . ." whispered Millie. "Oh, Sarah dear, what you've been through!"

"Don't remind her, Aunt Millie," William said briskly. "It's over now, and she's going to marry me and live happily ever after."

William grumbled that night after we were in bed when I told him we'd still have to wait a year after Henry's death before marrying; otherwise, I said, we'd leave ourselves open to criticism, and I wanted no more of that. And he wasn't too pleased when I said I'd invited Millie, Cousin Arthur, and Aunt Carrie to spend the rest of the summer in Oyster Bay.

"Am I never to have you to myself, Sarah darling?" he asked. "Are we to be saddled with them for the rest of our days? It isn't as if they were destitute; Aunt Carrie needs looking after, but the other two are perfectly competent. Arthur's just lazy."

"I know, William dear, but I can't leave them in the city for the hot weather, not when I have that lovely house. And Henry would have wanted me to take them in."

After a while he reluctantly agreed that it was the right thing to do, and said he'd go along with it provided he could have the room that adjoined mine, with the connecting door.

"Nora will feel evicted," I said to tease him.

"Let her," he murmured huskily, slipping my nightgown down from my shoulders.

"I have it all worked out, darling," William said the next morning while we were still in bed. "You've never said it, but I know you feel a repugnance toward this house; you can't sleep in your own room—and I don't blame you—no, don't speak. I'm going to sell it; we'll all go to Oyster Bay for the remainder of the summer. I'll commute to the office. Then in the fall Arthur can find a small flat; he can afford it now. Millie can take Aunt Carrie to live with her on Tenth Street, and you and I will find a place we like. How does that sound?"

"I like it; I think it's perfect, but are you sure the others will agree?"

"I don't see how they can object. Of course, we can invite them to visit in the summers . . ."

"Henry once suggested that we might live in Oyster Bay all year round. We could do that. Then, of course, there's my house in Gramercy Park. Would you consider that for the winter?"

"Anything you want, love, as long as we get out of here. Gramercy Park might be more convenient for me in bad weather, but you decide."

18

I took Nora back to Long Island with me the next day, leaving the others to close up the city house. I probably should have stayed and helped, but I wanted to open up the extra bedrooms in Oyster Bay and see that everything was in order for our visitors. At least that was the excuse I gave; in reality I couldn't wait to leave the gloomy brownstone, the house of murder, as I had come to think of it. As the taxi that took us to the station pulled away from the curb, I cast no backward glance at the dark facade, but stared straight ahead, hoping I would never see it again.

"Will you be wantin' me to sleep upstairs in the room next to yours, ma'am?" Nora asked when we were settled in our seats on the train. "Or shall I—"

"Just for a few nights, Nora," I replied. "I promised Mr. William you would. Then, when the others come, that will be his room. Do you mind?"

"Oh, no, ma'am. Of course not. But Cook and Bridget would think it funny if I wasn't sleepin' where I belong. So it's better that I put all my things in the servants' wing before they come."

What a careful little creature she was! And how sensible! Much as I'd hate to lose her, I found myself hoping she'd find happiness, if not with Joseph, then with someone else.

With her help I managed to have everything ready when

William arrived at the end of the week with Millie, Cousin Arthur, Aunt Carrie, Cook, and Bridget. They all seemed glad to be out of the city, and settled down almost immediately to the quiet routine of life in the country. William took a week's vacation, and then commuted daily to New York, Aunt Carrie fluttered about, dividing her time between her cat, whom Joseph had kept over the winter, and her flower arrangements, and Cousin Arthur occupied himself as usual with his books and papers. I didn't worry about either of them, but I was concerned about Millie, who seemed to withdraw into herself more and more as the summer progressed.

I guessed that Agatha's death had affected her more than it had the rest of us; after all, they'd lived together for almost half a century, and even if there had been no great love or affection between them, Millie must have felt some sense of loss. She would carry a book and a lawn chair down to a spot away from the house, from which she had a view of the water, and stay there for most of the day. Sometimes Cousin Arthur would join her, but whether they conversed or sat in silence, I did not know. I did notice, however, that she made a point of being freshly bathed and dressed by the time William came home, and I remember her delighted expression when he gave her a hug and teased her about getting fat from all the "loafing," as he called it. (She was almost painfully thin.)

I know now that I had reason to be concerned about her . . .

As soon as we returned to the city, William tried again to persuade me to marry him at once instead of waiting until February, when the official mourning period would be over. At first I demurred, but a short conversation with one of the denizens of Gramercy Park caused me to change my mind. My tenants had not been destructive, but a certain amount of painting and refurbishing had to be done before we could move into Number 17A, and I went down to check on the work from time to time. As I was leaving the house after conferring with the carpenter one afternoon, old Mrs. Ambrose, who lived next door to us, was emerging from her front door with her noisy little dog on a leash. Father had always thought her a busybody, and I generally kept my distance from her, but when she greeted me pleasantly and said she was delighted that I was returning to Gramercy Park, I had to stop for a moment.

"You'll be all alone, won't you, my dear?" she asked. "I read all about poor Mr. Cobb's tragic end."

"No, Mrs. Ambrose," I said quickly, without thinking. "My husband—"

"Oh, have you remarried so soon? Well, well! I'm happy for you, Sarah. I hope he's a good man."

"Yes, he's a splendid man. Please excuse me if I rush off; I'm late for an appointment."

I could almost feel her eyes boring into my back as I hurried over toward Fifth Avenue.

"William dear, you are going to have to marry me immediately, next week, or—" I said to him as soon as he came in that evening.

"What about tomorrow?" he asked with a smile as he put his arms around me. "Of course, of course, darling, but may I ask why the sudden rush?"

When I told him about Mrs. Ambrose, and about how I was afraid she'd cry out from the housetops that we were living in sin, he laughed and said he owed the lady a vote of thanks.

"Oh, she's an old gossip," I said. "A scandalmonger from

way back. You wouldn't like her at all. But there's another reason for a wedding. I'm pretty sure I'm pregnant."

"Oh, my darling! What great news! Do you feel all right? Here, sit down—no, let me hold you!"

19

Our baby, whom we named John Henry in honor of both of his grandfathers, was born early in May 1914, in the same room in which I had come into the world. He was pure joy from the moment of his arrival, and although we had a nurse, I reveled in caring for him myself, bathing him, dressing him, and wheeling him up and down the familiar paths inside the railings of the park. Cook and Bridget vied with each other for the privilege of holding him (Nora had married her Joseph the previous Christmas and gone to live in Oyster Bay), and I find it remarkable that Johnny wasn't completely spoiled in his infancy. He wasn't, though; he simply was a happy baby with a sunny disposition he was to retain for the rest of his life.

Once in a while I would intercept a curious glance from other frequenters of the park as I pushed the baby carriage along or sat on one of the benches rocking it gently. In my mind I could hear the passerby saying to herself, "Isn't she the one who—?" But that did not happen often, and as time went on, the glances changed to nods and smiles, and finally to "Good mornings" or "Good afternoons."

Our lives were quiet and fairly uneventful at the time. We did not go out in society; William had never cared for it, and I was just as glad to avoid elaborate, formal gatherings. Occasionally we went to a play or a motion picture; I remember seeing Jerome Kern's popular musical *The Girl from Utah*, and D. W. Griffith's *Birth of a Nation*, which took the city by storm. The "flickers," as the movies were called then, were just coming into their own, with Mary Pickford, Theda Bara, and the Gish sisters the favorites of the day. And of course there was Mack Sennett with his Keystone Comedies, as well as Charlie Chaplin, and poor Pauline and her perils—it all seems so innocent now.

At home we entertained infrequently, mostly at small dinner parties for William's colleagues and business acquaintances, or of course, at family birthday celebrations. Aunt Carrie, Millie, and Cousin Arthur, who were regular visitors, showered Johnny with toys. Since he had so many, enough to last him until he was ten, I was sure, I would have begged them to stop bringing the carefully chosen presents had I not felt saddened when Millie said that shopping for the baby helped pass the time, fill in her days with Aunt Carrie. Cousin Arthur had been the busy one; his biography of Robert E. Lee was finally finished and in the hands of the publisher. He was jubilant, and also touched that I gave a little dinner to celebrate the completion of the book.

"You can't know what a relief it is to have done with it after all this time," he said toward the end of the meal.

"What will you do next, Arthur?" I asked.

"Probably a book on Lincoln, his presidential years," he answered. "By the way, William, what has become of the medal and the Lincoln letter? I hope you didn't leave them in Henry's safe."

"Of course not," William answered shortly. "They're in the vault in the bank." He hated to be reminded of the Forty-ninth Street house, which had been sold to a midwesterner who had made a fortune in soap flakes. We were given to understand that his wife and daughters were anxious to enter into New York society, and wanted "a good address." They bought the house completely furnished, which spared us the trouble of disposing of its contents ourselves. None of us wanted any mementoes, although I did take the painting of the garden, and hung it over my father's old desk in the little library. I never did find out how Henry came by it.

I saw Millie studying it one rainy June afternoon when she brought Aunt Carrie over for tea, but she turned away from it without making any comment. I thought she was looking rather downcast that day, and was glad when Nurse Wilson brought Johnny in and put him in her outstretched arms. Her face lighted up, and she looked almost girlishly pretty as she talked softly to him. Then William appeared, and without a word she handed the baby over to me, and prepared to devote herself to her nephew.

"I was beginning to feel jealous of Johnny, Aunt Millie," William said after kissing me and touching the baby's cheek with a gentle finger. "I thought maybe he was displacing me in your affections."

"Nobody will ever do that, William, dear," she answered, patting his hand. "Nobody."

"And you, Aunt Carrie, am I still your favorite, too?" he asked, passing the sandwich plate to her.

"Oh, of course, William," she answered nervously, "but, then, I think maybe Sarah is . . ."

He laughed, sitting back in the armchair and crossing his legs. "Well, as long as it's Sarah, I won't make an issue of it. And I can't say I blame you."

Millie frowned, started to say something about the rainy weather, but stopped in midsentence and asked when we would be leaving for Oyster Bay.

"Oh, yes!" Aunt Carrie clapped her hands like a child. "My flowers! Sarah, you will let me do them again this year, won't you?"

"Of course I will," I answered. "And, Millie, we'll be out there by the end of the month. Can you be ready by then? William is arranging for a limousine to take us down."

We continued to spend our summers on Long Island, even after America entered the Great War in the spring of 1917. In view of his professional experience, William was commissioned a lieutenant and set to work in the office of the Army Engineers in Washington, D.C. He managed to come home every three or four weeks for a few days, and although life without him was lonely, I knew better than to complain; he could have been sent abroad.

Johnny at three was an active child, and needed constant watching, but fortunately Nora was more than willing to bring her round-faced little Billy over and supervise them both when I was busy. I think Nurse Wilson would have stayed on had I begged her, but I knew her heart was set on "doing her bit," as she called it, caring for wounded soldiers. Later on I received a letter from her from "somewhere in France," and a picture of her standing next to the ambulance she drove. I never heard, though, whether she returned safely or not.

I worked a few hours a week at the local chapter of the Red Cross, and would have spent more time there if I hadn't disliked being away from Johnny for any length of time. And I was beginning to think Millie needed watching, too; she seemed to be becoming more and more remote as time went on, although she was as sweet and affable as ever, and obviously doted on Johnny. She brushed aside my inquiries about her health, and after a while I stopped making them, although I thought she ought to see a doctor. If I had insisted on her seeking medical advice then, things might have been different, but maybe not: Millie's problem was not physical, as I soon learned.

20

If Aunt Carrie hadn't been worried about the garden, if Cousin Arthur, who was doing volunteer work in a recruiting office in the city, had not been down for the weekend, God alone knows what might have happened that Saturday night.

The sound of heavy rain beating against the house awakened me, and as I hurried into Johnny's room to close his window I heard the rumble of thunder in the distance. The little night-light on his chest of drawers cast only a dim glow, but enough so that the figure bending over his crib was clearly outlined. I must have gasped, because Millie turned around suddenly to face me, one hand on the side of the crib and the other in the pocket of her bathrobe.

"Oh, Sarah dear, you startled me! I just came in to see that little John was covered. He kicks off his blanket, you know. I wouldn't want my baby to take cold . . . I couldn't sleep, you see."

The rapid, disjointed way in which she spoke, and the nervous manner in which she kept fingering whatever was in her pocket, should have warned me that something was wrong, but at the time I was only interested in getting her out of the room before Johnny woke up.

"Come, Millie," I whispered. "I'll get you some warm milk. It will help you sleep." I took her gently by the arm and guided her toward the door.

Once out in the hall, she put her hand to her forehead for a moment, and then looked around vaguely as if she didn't know where she was.

"You get into bed, Millie, and I'll bring the milk up to you," I said, starting for the stairs. At that moment there was a brilliant flash of lightning, followed almost immediately by a series of thunderclaps, loud beyond any I ever heard. The lights flickered and went off completely, and then several things happened simultaneously. Aunt Carrie burst out of her room, crying that the garden would be ruined; Cousin Arthur appeared with a flashlight in his hand; the lights came back on again; and Millie stood as one transfixed, staring at me, and holding a pair of scissors in her hand.

"Millie, what on earth are you doing with my scissors?" Aunt Carrie wanted to know. "Surely you don't need them in the middle of the night."

"Give me the scissors, Millie," Cousin Arthur said, holding out his hand to take them from her. "There, that's a good girl,"

"I was just going to cut some flowers," Millie said in a faint, faraway voice as she turned toward her room. "But another day will do."

"She's been having a nightmare," Aunt Carrie whispered before trailing off toward her doorway.

"I'm not so sure it was a nightmare," Cousin Arthur muttered as he followed me down to the kitchen. "Sarah, have you noticed the change in Millie lately? So absent-minded—maybe she's gone round the bend."

While the milk was heating I told him about finding her in Johnny's room, and how strangely she spoke when she saw me.

"She kept her hand in her pocket, Arthur; I think she had the scissors in there. Could she have been going to cut off a lock of Johnny's hair, or . . ."

"Can't tell what she might have been going to do with those shears," he said. "I think she needs watching, Sarah.

Might do some harm to herself. I'll be here tomorrow, if you want me to keep an eye on her—stay over a few days if you like."

"Oh, Arthur, would you? William won't be home until next weekend; you'd be such a help."

"Of course, my dear," he answered. "Just have to make a phone call or two."

Millie was asleep when I went up with the milk, but I left it for her, and went to bed myself on a cot in Johnny's room. I slept poorly, haunted by the picture of Millie bending over the little boy's crib—and with those sharp scissors so close at hand! I wondered if she had made other nighttime visits to his room of which I was unaware. Would she hurt him? I wondered—and tried to assure myself that she was too fond of her great-nephew to do him an injury—but still . . . Her recent behavior and her crazy talk about cutting flowers in the dark made me uneasy, and before drifting off into a fitful sleep, I made up my mind to talk to Dr. Baldwin, whom I knew slightly from the previous summer when he had treated Johnny for a sore throat.

I was afraid Millie would protest when I told her I thought she needed a tonic, and that I had sent for the doctor, but she only looked at me strangely for a moment, and then said yes, maybe she did, and added that she hadn't been feeling too chipper lately. She thought she would stay in bed until the doctor had seen her. He came early in the afternoon when Johnny was napping, so I was able to talk to him alone after he made his examination.

"From what you've told me, Mrs. Cobb," he said, putting his satchel down and leaning against the railing on the verandah, "and from my own observations, I suspect that Miss Cobb is suffering from the onset of premature senility. I cannot, of course, be certain. If I were you, I would consult a specialist; I can give you the name of one. In the meantime, keep an eye on her; she might wander off or get into trouble. She had no recollection of having a pair of scissors in her possession, by the way."

"Is there any danger of her becoming violent?" I asked, thinking of the strange look I'd seen in her eyes when the lights came back on.

"It certainly is a possibility, Mrs. Cobb, although she seems too withdrawn at the moment. However, she does need supervision, and perhaps, in time, custodial care."

He gave me the name of a specialist in New York, and after I had talked the matter over with Cousin Arthur, who agreed to accompany Millie into the city, I called for an appointment first thing Monday morning. Unfortunately the doctor was on vacation, and would not be in the office until the following week. We could think of nothing else to do but to wait, and watch.

If Millie was aware that she was under constant surveillance, she showed no indication of it, nor did she ever refer to Dr. Baldwin's visit or to the events that had taken place on Saturday night. In fact, she seemed so much improved, so much like her old self, sweet, affable, agreeing readily to help with small chores, that I began to think she had made a complete recovery from whatever had been ailing her. And I well remember the joyous expression on her face when I reminded her on Thursday that William would be home the next day.

"Dear William," she said, smiling happily. "How good it will be to see him. I shall have to see if my blue dotted swiss is fresh; he's so fond of that dress, you know. He's such a dear boy. I'll just run upstairs now, and see if any of the buttons need tightening. I'll go right now, Sarah dear, if you don't need me."

I had to smile to myself as I watched her cross the lawn and go into the house, and wonder whether Dr. Baldwin could have been mistaken in his diagnosis. I found out the next day that he had not.

We frequently went down to the beach about eleven o'clock to have a swim before lunch. Nora and I had discovered that after an hour of play at the water's edge, the two little boys were more than ready for a hearty lunch and a long nap during the hot part of the day. That Friday Millie joined us, as she did occasionally. She was a far better swimmer than I was, having learned as a child, and would venture much farther from the shore than I ever dared. She and I played with Johnny and Billy for a while, and then, leaving them to Nora, went into the water.

Millie swam off by herself, and after practicing the breast-stroke for a few minutes, I turned over and floated content-edly on my back, closing my eyes against the glare of the August sun, listening to the squeals of Johnny and Billy as they splashed each other, and mentally counting the hours until William's arrival. I was wondering whether I'd have time to wash my hair when something caught hold of the back of my high-necked bathing dress and jerked my head under the water.

I do not know how long my panic-stricken struggle lasted, but I think I was on the verge of losing consciousness when the hold on me was released and I regained the surface, coughing and gasping for air. I heard Cousin Arthur say, "Steady, steady, Sarah, easy does it," and as he put his arm around me and helped me out of the water I could hear Millie's plaintive voice behind us.

"Oh, dear, dear Sarah—I'm so sorry—I never meant—I felt faint, and had such a cramp! I swam too far. I thought I was going to drown—and then I saw you and caught hold of you. Oh, dear, you saved my life! Are you all right? I wish . . . Oh, I'm afraid I must go up to my room . . ."

A frightened Nora rushed up to me with my beach towel and one of her own, which she wrapped around me with shaking hands, and Cousin Arthur sat down next to me on the warm sand, patting my shoulder reassuringly. When I felt that I was once more breathing normally, I turned to face him.

"Did Millie try—" I began.

"Without a doubt, Sarah," he said, nodding his head. "I was standing at the edge of the water—I'd been watching a sailboat disappear around the point—when I saw her swim toward you, and then dive under the water. A moment later you went down. Thank God I realized immediately that something was wrong! She still had hold of you when I got there . . ."

"What are we to do, Arthur? She said she felt faint, that she had a cramp. Maybe she panicked."

"We can't prove she didn't, Sarah, but I don't believe her for one minute. In any case, she's not all there, and may be unaccountable for her actions. We must convince William that arrangements should be made. God knows what, though."

William needed no convincing that Millie required special care; he arrived late in the afternoon, and as soon as he heard what had happened he was ready to cart her off immediately.

"But we can't be sure, William," I said. "She may really have felt faint."

"It makes no difference," he said, holding my hand firmly in his, "whether she knew what she was doing or not. You might have—oh, my darling, to think—no, she'll have to be put away, that's all there is to it."

Any doubts in our minds about Millie's sanity were

dispelled that night at dinner; she came down in a long-sleeved black silk, not the blue dotted swiss after all, and asked me to introduce her to our guest.

"It's William, Millie," I said. "Surely you recognize William, even if he is in uniform."

"William?" she asked vaguely. "Oh, yes, dear. William who?"

"Millie, for goodness' sake, you know our William," Aunt Carrie said with unusual asperity.

Millie looked at her and nodded, but said nothing further. During the meal she asked William twice what his name was, and as soon as we rose from the table, she extended her hand to him and graciously requested him to call again.

Through Dr. Gillespie and the specialist Dr. Baldwin had recommended, we were able to have Millie admitted to a private sanitarium in Greenwich, Connecticut. The matron told us she seemed to think she was a guest at a resort, and that the attendants were servants. Whenever I went to see her, she appeared to be content, yes, content, not happy. But then what real happiness had Millie ever known? I wonder. She never talked about herself . . .

When Millie died in the fall of 1923, I was in the hospital for the birth of our third child, Philip, and it was left to William to make the funeral arrangements. The case containing her personal belongings must have arrived at Gramercy Park before I returned home with our new baby, because I never saw it until last spring when we were preparing for the permanent move to Oyster Bay. William, who had been working long hours at the time, had had it carried up to the storeroom on the top floor and forgot to mention it. It stayed there, untouched, for more than twenty-five years.

"Of course," William said when we opened the case and saw the note from Matron resting on top of Millie's neatly folded old-fashioned dresses, "I remember now: it arrived when Philip was born, and I didn't want to bother you with it when you came home from the hospital—I completely forgot about it. It's rather late in the day to answer Matron's letter, isn't it? But what does she say?"

"Dear Mr. and Mrs. Cobb," I read. "Here are Miss Millie's things, which I think you will find in perfect order. She kept her clothes so neat. I am happy to tell you that the end was peaceful; she died in her sleep and when we found her she was even smiling. Ever so sweet Miss Millie was, right to the end."

"Poor Millie," William said, "what a boring life she must have had. What will we do with this stuff?"

"I'll go through it, William, and if there's nothing worth saving, I'll have to throw it all away. No one could possibly use these clothes today," I said, picking up one garment after the other. "Look, here's the diary you gave her one Christmas. And she's written in it. Do you want to see it?"

"Not now, darling. Put it aside and I'll look at it some other time. No, let me take it downstairs and pack it in one of the cartons of books."

When I went into the library a little while later, however, William was sitting in my father's old easy chair, staring out the window, with the little blue leather book in his hand.

"I think you'd better read this, Sarah," he said, holding it out to me, "and tell me what you think. Read it aloud, darling; I want to be sure I didn't miss anything."

PART THREE

Millie

1

I understand only too well what Henry David Thoreau meant when he wrote about men leading lives filled with quiet desperation, for during the years after William's birth, when I was forced to watch him mature from a distance, my life was indeed quietly desperate. At some point, though, and it was many years before this happened, built-up resentment and anger caused my personality to change, and my mind to be constantly filled with thoughts of revenge and retribution.

By the time Maria died Henry was a man of great wealth, and up until his marriage to Sarah Cunningham I felt confident that William would be his heir. But suppose Sarah and Henry had a child? A son of his own would inevitably take precedence over an adopted bastard. Or suppose he left it all to Sarah? He was besotted enough with her to do just that. Oh, I haven't words to express the fury I felt (a fury I kept well hidden) every time I saw Henry with her, caressing her with his eyes, and no doubt longing to do so with his hands. He lavished everything on her, catered to her slightest whim, gave her jewels, furs, trips abroad, whatever he thought would please her.

I do not believe I begrudged her all the luxuries Henry heaped on her, but when I realized she was entrapping

William; I became almost frantic. To think of it! Not content with my brother, she wanted my son as well, and to make matters worse, I could see that William was more than willing to be entrapped. Aggie was not far off the mark when she questioned the propriety of the two of them strolling arm in arm in the park, but unfortunately that remark caused Henry to fly into a temper and put her out of the house. His beloved Sarah could do no wrong.

I, on the other hand, could do nothing at all, either right or wrong; my hands were tied, and as time went on, the wound that Henry and Maria had dealt me in taking William from me festered and gnawed. I wanted revenge: I wanted to have William to myself, and I wanted to secure for him the entire fortune that Henry would eventually bequeath. My brother would, in all likelihood, predecease Sarah; he was, after all, thirty years her senior. From the way he was behaving toward her, though, it seemed to me probable that she would inherit the bulk of his considerable estate. I needed to know what his plans were, and after turning the matter over and over again in my mind, I decided to enlist Aggie's help.

As I said earlier, my sister was greedy; she wasn't too bright, though, and I am sure she had no idea I was furthering my own ends when I brought up the subject of Henry's will.

"I wonder if Henry will leave everything to Sarah," I said idly one snowy evening as I watched Aggie help herself to a large piece of mince pie and cover it with hard sauce.

"All that money, Millie?" She sounded indignant. "He wouldn't dare! Why, most of it came from Papa, and should come to us, not to an outsider. I shall speak to Henry, ask him about his will; we might easily outlive him. Would he leave anything to William, do you think? After all, he's not . . ."

"I know, Aggie," I said, thinking she was playing right

into my hands. "The proper thing, of course, would be for him to leave it all to you and me, with an annuity or trust fund for Sarah." I stopped, letting the seed I had sown take root in her mind, knowing that she would not be satisfied until she found out the terms of the will.

Events moved quickly after that conversation, very quickly. The snow that had been falling that night had stopped by the time I looked out my window in the morning, and the temperature had dropped well below freezing. Henry slipped on the ice on his front stoop, and when he was recovering from the fall, he died suddenly from an overdose of laudanum. Sarah was accused of murdering him, put in prison, tried, and acquitted, but her reputation suffered. She was driven to seek seclusion in Oyster Bay, where she stayed until one hot day in July when William, in his determination to clear her name, set up that ridiculous reenactment of the night of Henry's death, and caused Aggie to die.

Sarah inherited half of the estate—just as much as William, which I thought most unfair, but I could see no way of contesting the will. I toyed with the idea, now that both Henry and Aggie were gone, of revealing the truth of his identity to William, but decided against doing it, at least for the time being. After all, I had no way of proving he was my son. Henry had seen to it that his birth was registered under the name of William Walker Cobb, and since Aggie was dead, there was absolutely no one to support my claim. Then, too, the revelation that he was illegitimate might turn him completely against me, and I couldn't bear that. I loved him far too dearly.

No, I had no love for Sarah, but I could not prevent William from marrying her; had I objected to the match, I might have alienated him. He was as much, if not more, in love with her than Henry had been, and would have married her no matter what I said. And I would have been left to my own devices.

As it was, I was pretty much alone anyway for the next few years; living with Aunt Carrie was more peaceful than it had been with Aggie, but hardly stimulating. I had hoped to move in with them in Gramercy Park, where I could be close to my grandson (how delightfully ironic it is that they inadvertently named him for his *real* grandfather!), but no invitation was forthcoming. At least I had the summer months with little John for a while, but that came to an end, all because I was not as careful as I should have been.

It's pleasant enough here in Greenwich, and I cannot complain that I am not well cared for. I'm not sure what this place really is, a sanitarium or a private hospital for elderly gentlewomen, but I pretend I think I am at a resort. After what happened in Oyster Bay it became necessary for me to pretend more than ever, to act somewhat queer, for my own protection.

You see, Arthur *knew* that I had tried to drown Sarah, and he looked at me so strangely the night I wanted to cut off a lock of little John's hair. I think he became suspicious then. He's not stupid, and it would not have taken him long to figure out that it was I, not Aggie, who killed Henry. In a way, I killed my sister, too; I'll come to that later.

First Henry: I must have been more than slightly irrational that night (I may not have been completely over my illness) when the thought of pouring the whole bottle of laudanum into his water occurred to me.

It's strange, isn't it, how a few hurtful words can set off a whole chain of events? And Henry uttered those words. Had he been kinder when I looked in on him that afternoon, I might not have taken the steps I did, at least not then, but he cut me down so roughly that I still smart when I think of it. The door to his room was ajar, but even so, I knocked softly before pushing it all the way open.

I could hear the sound of water running in the adjacent bathroom, the door to which had been left open, and assumed that Sarah was replenishing Henry's carafe, since the nurses had gone by then. My brother was sitting in the large leather armchair near the window, with an afghan over his legs, looking quite comfortable, I thought. When he saw me, however, a look of annoyance flashed across his face, and without a greeting of any kind, he lashed out at me.

"What are you pussyfooting around for, Millie?" he said crossly. "What do you want now? Haven't I done enough for you? When am I to have my home and my wife to myself?"

Humiliated, I turned and fled up to the fourth floor. I spent the rest of the afternoon alone in the little room that had been my son's night nursery, stung to the quick, and letting the resentment I felt for Henry build up in me until I was as one possessed. I replayed in my mind, over and over again, the scenes that had taken place when I was pregnant with William until I worked myself up into such a rage against Henry and his dead wife as I had never known, and by the time the early winter dusk had fallen, I had made up my mind, for good or evil, to even the score.

I had seen Dr. Gillespie give Sarah the little bottle of laudanum, and it was not difficult for me to find it in the drawer of the table next to her bed. I had a bad moment, though, when she came out of Henry's room and saw me going upstairs to the fourth floor just after I had come from her room, where I had carefully, without spilling a drop, substituted water for the laudanum. Yet she seemed to

173

believe me (how annoyingly trusting that woman is!) when I said I was tired and wanted to retire early. I guess it seemed reasonable, since I had been ill.

The rest was easy: I undressed and waited until I was sure everyone was asleep, and then went quietly down to the floor below, my velvet slippers making no sound on the carpeted stairs. Fortunately the water glass was not filled to the brim, and there was plenty of room for the contents of the little bottle I carried in my pocket. Henry did not stir, and minutes later I was back in my room, with no one the wiser.

Once in bed, though, I could not sleep. What on earth would I do, I wondered, if Sarah began to suspect me before I could replace the laudanum from the bottle we kept in the Tenth Street house for Aggie's headaches? I had heard Sarah say she didn't like the effect laudanum had on her, but that was no guarantee that she wouldn't take some if she had a wakeful night. And then, when it had *no* effect . . .

I hadn't anticipated that eventuality, but I didn't panic; I simply decided I could leave nothing to chance.

Neither of the attempts I made on Sarah's life was successful. The first time the loud click of the doorknob frightened me, and the second time the strength of my arms failed me when I tried to hold the pillow over her head. Perhaps I was somewhat stiff from crouching in the bottom of the linen closet in the bathroom for so long.

My hopes revived when Sarah was arrested for murdering Henry and taken to prison, where I thought she might die, prison conditions being what they were. In that case, with Henry and Sarah both gone, my son would inherit everything and I would have him to myself.

Things did not work out that way, though, and I was thoroughly frightened when I realized that William and

Sergeant Shaw had set a trap to catch Henry's murderer. I guess nothing would have come of their plan if I had not suggested to Aggie that she might take advantage of the opportunity to search Henry's room for the Lincoln medal. I told her that by rights, it was ours, and she agreed, saying she wondered why she hadn't thought of that herself. I didn't expect her to go look for it in the middle of the night, though; just before breakfast the next day would have been more sensible. She could have been late coming down, you see, and no one would have been the wiser.

Poor Aggie! She wasn't a very nice person, but she was innocent of the crime everyone thought she had committed. Shaw was satisfied, and the case was closed once and for all. They even thought she had made the attack on Sarah, the poor fools.

I did nothing for the next few years, but the thought of getting rid of Sarah was never far from my mind. I was sure that if she were out of the way, William would naturally ask me to move in with him and take care of little John. If only Arthur had been engrossed in his books instead of looking out over the water that day . . .

It's all over now, and I am safe here, but when Sarah and William come to visit me I have to be very careful to pretend to remember nothing about those last days in Oyster Bay. They will be here next Saturday, I am told, and it will be so very, very good to see my dear boy. I wish they'd bring little John with them; he is seven now, just the age his father was when I had him to myself for a fortnight. Perhaps they don't allow children here, though. I've never seen my granddaughter, Angela, who must be two or three by this time. Maybe Sarah will have a picture of her; I'd like to see if she resembles me, and if she has John Townsend's eyes.

I haven't been easy in my mind lately, but perhaps I'll feel better now that I've put all this down in the little blue leather diary William gave me last Christmas. Maybe it's true that confession is good for the soul . . .

EPILOGUE

Sarah

We didn't speak for a few moments when I finished reading. I found it difficult to think coherently, and I suspected William was having the same trouble. Was Millie really a murderess, or had she imagined it? I asked myself, and then I remembered that she *did* try to drown me. I can't forget that, or how at the time we blamed the episode on a deranged mind. Was she ever really crazy? And why did she think William was her son? Could it be true that he was, and that she loved him enough to kill for him? Would I be driven to commit murder if someone took one of my babies away from me? So many questions—and no answers . . .

Somehow we got through the rest of the day and the night that followed, although neither of us slept well. We had stayed up late discussing what Millie had written, wondering how much, if any, of it was true, and if she meant us to find the diary or if she had intended to destroy it before she died.

The next morning William was unusually quiet, and left the house right after breakfast, saying he needed a good long walk. When he returned shortly before noon I was in the library taping up the last of the cartons, and one glance at his face assured me that his mind was at rest, that he had come to some sort of decision.

He picked the diary up from where it lay on the table in front of the sofa, and stared at it for a moment.

"As far as this is concerned, Sarah," he said slowly, tapping the leather cover with his index finger, "we have two choices: either to believe that this is the truth, or to believe that it is all the product of a mind that became unhinged that summer when she grabbed you in the water. And either way, I don't see that it matters now. Everyone concerned in the events of 1913 is dead and gone, you and I have had thirty-five years of marital happiness, and nothing that Millie wrote can take that away. Nor does it matter whose son I am; perhaps she did have an affair and I am the product of it. I don't know and I don't care. I choose to believe that Henry and Maria Cobb were my parents, but maybe they weren't. I'm certainly not going on any Freudian search for my identity. It makes no difference in our lives, darling, who begot me. And as far as Pa's death is concerned, the law can't touch either Aggie or Millie now."

With that he tore the pages from the binding of the diary and watched them flare up in the fire that had burned low. Then he threw the leather cover in the trash basket next to the desk and said there was just time for a glass of sherry before lunch.

Since that day, ten years ago now, William has never referred to the diary; he appears to have dismissed it from his mind completely. Of course I never mention it, and I seldom think about it, but one afternoon recently when I happened to look out at the lawn that slopes so gently down to the bay, I could almost see Millie sitting quietly in the warm sun, an un-opened book in her lap. Suddenly I was reminded of the last words of Matron's note to us: "Ever so sweet Miss Millie was, right to the end."

I shivered slightly, then turned quickly away from the window and went down to the verandah, where William was reading one of my little stories to our youngest granddaughter. Her name is Sarah Anne, and William thinks she resembles me.